"Like the author, Annie D. is such a mesmerizing storyteller that you can almost feel the fire at your back."

The New York Times Book Review

"A quietly confiding first novel about domestic tragedies and village violence."

The Kirkus Reviews

"A clear, dry voice, stripped of sentiment or passion, narrates an absorbing saga of love, madness and murder.... This authentically and distinctively cadenced first novel marks a promising debut."

Publishers Weekly

"Chehak's prose provides a seamless, calm flow to a novel whose elements of love and murder ripple enticingly, fully surfacing only gently, only eventually, in the most satisfying kind of storytelling."

Booklist

THE STORY OF ANNIE D.

Susan Taylor Chehak

FAWCETT CREST • NEW YORK

For Tom

RIDEMUS ET AMAMUS

Contents

1

The D in Annie D.

O FORTUNATOS NIMIUM,
SUA SI BONA NORINT, AGRICOLAS

There was no way Daniel Shires could have known that the river which cut so conveniently through the eighty acres of Nebraska farmland that he chose to homestead back in 1859 was only running so high and wide that spring because it was flooded. By summertime, when the heat was on and the prairie grasses began to burn, that river, which was to become the same deceptive body of water after which the town of Wizen River would take its name, had dried up and dwindled to a creek.

But Daniel Shires had come far enough. He would not be moving on.

He had fled famine, death, and disease, along with many thousands of other optimistic emigrants, to settle in the vast and reportedly prosperous American wilderness. His less robust wife had been unable to survive even the rough ocean crossing, and so it was Daniel and his son, Weary, who traveled by prairie schooner across the plains to Nebraska.

By the time that the river underwent its unfortunate metamorphosis, Daniel had his house half built and his fields plowed and planted. It was too late then to do any

1

more exploring. He and Weary had acres of rich and fertile soil to cultivate and call their own, and they were not about to give it all up to go off in search of a real river. The creek would have to do.

It couldn't have been easy for them. Even now, with thermostats and central air, fire houses and flood control, electricity and television, the people of Nebraska are still at the mercy of their climate. We talk about the weather as if she were a crazy queen—unpredictable and difficult to please.

Winters are bitter and unremitting; sometimes the mercury will not creep up above 10 below for weeks on end. Snow falls down and then piles up or blows off to form mammoth drifts. Whopping chunks of hail can knock a man unconscious, kill a prize hog, destroy a bumper crop.

With spring comes melted snow, and the rains that fall and flood the plains. Quiet little creeks become rampant rivers, precious topsoil gets swept away, plows and tractors become mired and are left abandoned in the hopelessly muddy fields.

Then summer rolls in, and with it the dog days that so thicken the air with heat and moisture that only the gnats and mosquitoes have the energy to whiz and bite. Thunderstorms ravage the night, a terror to children and livestock; stupendous twisters tear through the towns and visit disaster down upon the jerry-built trailer parks; fires catch the fields, whipped up and carried out of control by ruthless winds.

Plenty of other settlers sickened and died out there on the prairies. But Daniel and Weary Shires were intrepid; somehow they managed to survive and thrive.

Weary was my grandfather. He and his father built themselves a working farm out of those eighty acres, and when Daniel at last succumbed, Weary buried him on the slope behind the house and went on to work his land alone. In 1889, Weary married the daughter of a prosperous neighbor, and with his bride came one hundred and sixty more acres of land to call his own. Lucy was only eighteen when she and Weary were wed—he was fifty, a shrewd man

2

who was able to charm his way into possession of a pretty young bride and more than triple his property holdings in one swift bargain—and she spent the next ten years bearing and raising his seven children, six boys and, at last, in 1899, a girl, my mother, Mona Shires.

I have a single photograph, an old tintype, of my mother when she was a child, dressed up in all the frills and curls her small femininity could bear, surrounded by her bigger and more rugged brothers, held in her father's lap, the obvious pet of his affection. And there is Weary, as wizened as the river, grinning—a slash of toothless smile that stretches across his face from one ear to the other and that, at second glance, looks more like a grimace than a grin, an expression more of pain than of joy, less of pleasure than endurance.

Of all those six strapping sons, Weary couldn't manage to keep even one of them at home to work the land that he and Daniel Shires had homesteaded together back in 1859. The age of industry had come clanking in, and one by one each boy grew up and took off out of Nebraska. Some found jobs and money. One ended up in jail. Another went crazy and died. Only Mona, imprisoned by her girlishness and all the helplessness that it implied, was left.

If there was ever anything at all that Mona Shires dreamed of and prayed for, it was that there would come a time when she, too, would be allowed to veer away from her father's footsteps and follow in her brothers', away from the tedium and drudgery of a farmer's life and into a more civilized world, where a person didn't have to do battle with the elements day after day after day.

"Suffering and pain," she'd murmur, washing the blood from her hands after helping the men deliver a still-born breech calf. They wrapped a chain around its legs and cranked the calf, inch by inch, out into the world. "Who needs it?" She'd bang her pots and pans on the kitchen counter and break her dishes on the floor. "Please, God . . ."

As it turned out, her prayers weren't answered until many

years later, when I had already grown up and married and was about to become busy raising children of my own.

While Mona Shires was enduring her childhood in Wizen River, watching her aging father and her more independent brothers struggle to make a decent living on that land and seeing those brothers each one give up on the whole enterprise and take off to make a better life for himself elsewhere, a boy named Harley Plant was growing up in Chicago, dreaming of his own release, from the squalor and anonymity of the city to the cleaner and closer freedom of the farm. And when he returned from his tour of duty as an Army private in World War I, older and wiser and more anxious than ever to leave civilization to the savages, he came to Nebraska as a salesman, peddling Bibles and calendars and greeting cards and paper-covered novels to farmers and their families across the state.

His route took him through Wizen River, and it was there that he met Mona Shires. She let him sell her not one but two of his most expensive Bibles, and she bore the wrath of Weary Shires when he learned of her extravagance.

When Harley Plant passed through Wizen River a second time, Mona was waiting for him. She began her conquest in earnest then, browsing through his books, giving him coy looks and pretty poses, purchasing several sets, and at last becoming so bold as to invite him up to the porch for a little lemonade and cake.

That was the beginning of a courtship that would last a full year, picking up where it had left off once every two weeks, when Harley Plant passed through Wizen River again.

The year was 1920. Weary Shires gave away the hand of his only daughter to Harley Plant in the same old Episcopal church in Wizen River where Weary and Lucy Shires had been married and would be eulogized, where I was christened and later wed, and where my own two boys were also christened and later laid out. And then he took the bride and groom back to his farmhouse to drink a toast to their union.

4

The plan was that the newlyweds would honeymoon in Chicago where Harley would then take up a job as office manager for the company that had sent him out to sell their books in the first place. Mona had already packed her bags in anticipation of her release, and she was anxious to be off when Weary—was it with a grimace or a grin?—threw a wrench into the works by taking Harley aside at the last minute and offering him full ownership of the farm.

Lock, stock, and barrel.

Now Weary knew that Harley wouldn't be able to turn down such a promising prospect. And so while Mona raved and cried and hurled curses—and dishes and whatever else she could find that was handy to smash—at her father, Weary accepted Harley's gratitude for that unexpected dowry and then, with a knowing wink, sent him on upstairs to soothe his infuriated bride.

Whatever it was that Harley did up there, it worked just as Weary had known it would, and an hour later, when he and Mona descended the stairway from their bedroom to the parlor, Mona was quiet and flushed and clinging to Harley.

They did go to Chicago, and they did spend some time there with his family. But then Harley informed the book company that he wouldn't be working for them anymore, and he and Mona packed back up and came home again to the farm in Wizen River. There they took up housekeeping with Mona's parents, in the old house which had, over the years, been expanded and modernized since Daniel Shires had first built it in 1859.

Mona was back where she had started, no match for both her husband's and her father's wills, married to a man who was no redeemer after all, but only a simple, gentle farmer, another fool like her father, who took pleasure in battling the elements just to bring forth some sustenance from the soil.

Harley was, in fact, a sorry sort of farmer, but he was determined, and he got by. He and Mona raised hogs and corn and chickens, all under the watchful tutelage of a more experienced, but less chipper, Weary.

5

And then, in 1921, I was born, the product of that first pacification that my father had worked upon his bride on the afternoon that they were married. Two years later, resting easy now that he had at last got himself a son, albeit in law, to take over for him, Weary Shires gave up the ghost and passed over in his sleep. Lucy Shires stayed on with us, helping Mona keep house and advising Harley when she could, until she, too, was gone, when I was nine. We buried her up on the slope behind the house, next to Daniel and Weary Shires.

And with her mother's passing, Mona's fate was sealed.

What Harley Plant lacked in experience, he more than made up for in sheer strength and tenacity. He just would not let anyone or anything get him down. He was a huge, clumsy, ruggedly handsome man, all muscle and denim and sweat, and he could lift me up and toss me around like an old, but treasured, sack of potatoes.

Nevertheless, Mona was determined that I wouldn't follow in her footsteps to become just another poor farm girl up to her knees in mud and muck. She saw to it that I was educated, and she gave me all the manners and grace of what she considered to be a real lady.

While Harley was out in the weather planting his corn or mending his fences, Mona and I were in the parlor, stitching pretty samplers or tatting dainty linens. I would look up from my small work to see Harley out there in his fields, his yellow hair blown all wild, as he struggled to make our old rusty tractor pull the plow through the heavy soil.

Every day I had to do extra lessons. Mona was sure that I would never be near pretty enough for my looks alone to bring about the fulfillment of all her hopes and dreams, and so she took it upon herself to teach me, besides my regular schoolwork, to read and write in Latin. She thought that maybe that would somehow make me more attractive to a gentleman who didn't have his hands in the dirt.

Together we went through our conjugations and declensions—nominatives and ablatives, objectives and subjunctives, pluperfects and future perfects, gerund and participle, number and case—and then Harley would come stomping in and shoo me off to change out of my crisp little dress and into overalls and boots. He and I would trudge out into the snow or rain or heat to slop the hogs while Mona made thunder in the kitchen, taking all her rage and frustration out on those poor old banged-up pots and pans.

When I was seventeen, the boys should have begun to come around. But they never did. Instead, I had become a sort of a joke in Wizen River, partly because those boys were afraid of me—what one of them could ever hope to find anything at all to say to a girl who knew how to sew doilies and translate Virgil?—and partly because the girls thought that I was odd and strange and different from any of them, and mostly because they all together believed that I held myself up as just too good for any of them, which wasn't true at all.

It was Mona who put on airs, not me, and not Harley.

If it hadn't been for Phoebe, I wouldn't have had any friends at all.

Phoebe's father owned the bank, and Mona thought that that was fine.

We were just out of high school when the war came along, and then all the boys, including Jack Tooker, went away to make heroes of themselves by fighting off the Germans and the Japs. Phoebe would come to visit in the evening and we would listen to the war news on the radio. She'd wring her hands and get all red-eyed with worry about whether Jack was going to get himself killed over there.

Phoebe had dropped out of high school to marry Jack, and she loved the drama of her situation. She looked to tragedy to give her meaning all her life. Maybe she cared more about Jack when he was gone than she would have if he had still been there with her at home, where nothing bad could happen to him, and it was safe.

We worked together for the Women's Relief Club. One of our projects was to set up tables in the train station, and a phonograph playing all the most popular records, and when the trainloads of boys came through we danced with them and gave them coffee and little snacks that we had baked ourselves.

I did a lot of baking, but not much dancing. Phoebe danced, and she told me that she always pretended that the boy who held her was Jack, returned safe and sound from his fighting, maybe wounded, quiet and strong.

And then the war was over, and Jack did come back home to Phoebe, and Phoebe was pregnant. She lost that baby, miscarried it, and didn't get pregnant again with Lacey until four years later.

I was there in my parlor, twenty-seven years old, still stitching and reading and conjugating verbs, keeping myself so busy that a local boy wouldn't have touched me with a ten-foot pole.

That was when Dr. Diettermann showed up, not exactly a knight on a stallion, but a liberator nonetheless. He came to Wizen River to take over the practice of our own aging doctor, and everybody was glad to have him, even if he was a German and couldn't speak much English at all.

And when Mona, who was always on the lookout for a man who she thought would be suitable—good enough, rich enough, educated and refined enough to court me—heard that there was a new doctor who was sorely in need of an English teacher, she had just the girl for him.

Little Annie Plant.

Mona arranged everything, and Dr. Diettermann drove out to our farm once a week to learn to speak the language. Now, although Mona and I both, she as my instructor and I as her pupil, could read and write Latin with some proficiency, neither of us had ever attempted to learn German. I tried to explain to Mona that there was no connection whatsoever between the two, but she only got cross and told me that if I couldn't work with words, then maybe I should try pictures.

"Pictures?"

"Ja," said Mona, frowning, "ja, ja, ja!"

Dr. Diettermann stood in the doorway with his hat under his

arm, bowing and smiling and clicking his teeth. He reached out to shake my hand, and I remember that I noticed then how clean and smooth and soft his fingers felt next to mine.

I did as I was told. The Doctor and I spent our weekly hour at the table in the kitchen, passing drawings back and forth, trying to make sense of each other's words.

I drew a house.

"House," I said.

"Haus," the Doctor answered, smiling, pleased. He made the word sound like a sneeze.

He drew a tree.

"Baum," he said.

"Bomb?"

I pointed to the things in the kitchen. "Stove," I told him, "sink, icebox, counter, table, water . . ."

"Vasser," he said, clapping his hands. "Vodder."

"Wuh . . . wuh . . . wuh . . . water. Not vodder. Nein vodder. Wuh . . . wuh . . . wuh . . . water!"

"Ja! Vodder! Vuh . . . vuh . . . vuh . . . vodder!"

"Chair . . . hand . . . foot . . . leg . . . knee . . ."

This went on for almost six months. And then one evening, after we had carried on one of our first successful conversations all in English, the Doctor handed me a picture he had drawn. In it was a house.

"Haus!" he said, pointing and nodding.

The upstairs wall was missing, exposing the room. In the room was a bed.

"Bed!"

And on the bed were a man and a woman.

"Vooman!"

One on top of the other.

Across the bottom he had written, "Willst du meine Frau werden?"

I was blushing so hard that I was dizzy, and his round white face seemed to wobble and float, a balloon on a string, dreamlike and unreal before my eyes.

Never mind that Dr. Diettermann was a Kraut. Never mind that he was ten years older than me.

Dr. Diettermann had asked me to be his wife.

I wouldn't be an old maid after all, and I wouldn't be a farmer either. I would move into town and live in a proper house as the wife of the town doctor.

In 1949, I became Annie Diettermann, and I set up housekeeping with my husband in the Doctor's big house downtown.

And then, six months later, I was pregnant with Gunar, and Mona left.

She had done her job, seen to it that I was taken care of, and what else was there. She packed up her things and took off out of Wizen River, looking for something better, in search of a life that was more, and we never did hear one word from her again.

Maybe she's in New York, one of those wretched old women who carry everything they own around in plastic trash bags and call the subway station home. Maybe she's in an institution, a ward of the state. Or maybe she's dead. Anyway, she's not on the farm anymore.

Several years after that Harley died, quietly, in his sleep, dreaming, I expect, of weather and dirt and the good, warm blessing of the sun, and then the land that Daniel Shires had found at the end of his journey to America became mine. Dr. Diettermann got a good price for it. The men who bought it came in with their bulldozers and leveled the old house, and then they planted corn up where the Shireses and my father lay.

It was Phoebe who got everyone started calling me Annie D. It was quite a happy little joke to her that after all those years I had at last hooked myself a husband, and a doctor at that, and so she couldn't keep from always saying, "Why, hello there, Annie Diettermann!" putting just the slightest stress on the Diettermann. And then that got to be tiresome, so she shortened it to Annie D. And that's what they all still call me, even though the Doctor has been gone now for a long, long time.

And he never was able to get his *w*'s quite right.

2

Your Mother Is Dead.
I'm Sorry

OBIT

Whether she ever knew it or not, Phoebe Tooker had been promising, predicting, and even anticipating her own end for many years before she died. She would say to me, during those times when we talked over coffee about ourselves and our husbands and our children and our friends, that if one thing—and that was an understood reference to her thankless and delinquent daughter Lacey—didn't do her in, then another—her equally wayward and ungrateful husband Jack—would be pretty much bound to do the trick just as well.

And then she would shake her head, showing well enough how helpless she felt, and yet unable to resist taking it just one step further, exaggerating herself, becoming almost comic and even a little grotesque, by rolling her eyes so far back up into their sockets that the pretty blue irises disappeared altogether and all you saw was the red-flecked whites.

Like a person having a seizure. Like someone in the middle of a fit.

As it turned out, neither of those particular two of

Phoebe's worst and most unrelenting antagonists had anything at all to do with how she really died. Jack Tooker had left Phoebe, divorced her, and then been killed himself, ten years before the accident happened, and Lacey was so long gone that Phoebe hadn't had word or sight of her in nine.

It was that car, the one that Jack and Phoebe had been so proud of back when Lacey was still the baby that everybody loved the best, and before Phoebe had become a grousing malcontent.

It was a 1955 Chevy Bel Aire Nomad wagon, two-tone, with blue around the doors and fenders and white across the top.

"The latest thing," Jack had said, again and again. He was pretty proud of it and of the fact that it belonged to him, besides. He liked cruising up and down the streets of Wizen River, one arm flung back over the seat, the other hand hanging on the steering wheel, his gold wedding band glinting in the sunshine. Or he would fold his hands back behind his head, steering with his knee against the wheel, scaring Phoebe so until she screeched and buried her face in her hands.

"I can't look! I don't want to die! The baby, Jack . . . please!"

And Jack would laugh. He took a lot of pleasure out of teasing Phoebe that way. I think it made him feel powerful and strong to hear her whimper and cry and squeal, helpless and afraid like that. Probably she thought so, too.

That was sort of the way that Jack and Phoebe fit together all around. Where he was loud and brash, she would be timid and still. Where he was tall, long-legged, and lank, all smiles and jokes and fun, she was small and serious and afraid. Phoebe had to sit on a pillow to drive that car, and still she could barely see over the top of the wheel. And her feet barely even reached the pedals.

"Totally automatic," Jack would say, buffing a fender with the corner of one of Lacey's thick cotton diapers. "Practically drives itself."

The Tooker Place was once a noble old house, but by the

time that Phoebe was killed, what with its peeling paint and all those weeds, it had become an ordinary, rundown-looking thing. And the way down the hill into Wizen River had always been particularly dreadful for Phoebe. She didn't care one bit for the ditches that fell away with hardly a shoulder at all into the woods on either side of the road. Maybe it was picturesque, but she had to be always fighting the crazy impulse to turn off and drive right on over into them.

Or, anyway, that was what she said.

But no one, not the people that she pestered to put up some kind of a barricade along the shoulder, not Lacey, not Jack, and least of all myself, her closest friend and confidante, accustomed to the hyperbole of her many afflictions, had ever taken her seriously when she tried to describe that temptation toward self-destruction and the tremendous amount of willpower that it took for her to resist and keep the car on the road and gliding down that smooth plane of asphalt into town. With her steady accretion of grievances over the years, Phoebe had lost her credibility long before she came up with that one particular phobia.

And I guess the old car didn't help the situation much, either.

It was springtime, May, when the early morning warmth is so welcome, a vague hint of the swelter in the summer days to come. Phoebe was on her way down to visit with me, and she was at the wheel of that Chevy. She wouldn't sell it. She refused time and time again to try and have it traded in for a newer, smaller, more economical and less clumsy car. Phoebe was little, and dainty, and shy, but that was not to be confused with being weak.

It was Lacey who later came up with the whole idea that what had really happened was that her mother had swerved to avoid a stray dog in the road and then just kept on going, right on over the edge. The car climbed an oak tree and then fell back down into the ditch, belly up and wheels still spinning. Phoebe Tooker was tossed around inside that

Chevy—broken and torn to pieces—just like an old rag doll.

But Lacey—who came and gave us her own less complicated, more humane answer to what everybody was asking, which was how exactly did that Chevy end up upside down in the ditch?—seemed to know a whole lot more about it than any of the rest of us, including the authorities whose job it was to investigate the accident and take all those photographs of the scene. There was never any mention made in their reports of an animal in the road. It was pretty clear to them that Phoebe Tooker had turned the wheel and driven right off the shoulder. Just like that.

Kaboom . . . crash!

Maybe she'd been trying to steer the darned thing with her knee.

Nobody was able to give Lacey an explanation that she could appreciate. Or live with. Or understand or accept or pass on as being a true account of what had really happened.

Maybe she didn't like the idea that her mother had finally succumbed to the enticement of the ditches. She couldn't, even after the fact, bring herself to believe that the temptation that her mother had described often enough to harden us all had ever been a real one—the single one, in fact, of Phoebe's many neuroses that had been genuine enough to finally do her in.

But isn't it better in the end to admit to even the most unpleasant reality than to go on beguiling yourself with a more comfortable camouflage of the truth?

I would have to say so. And I butted in and tried to tell Lacey about how the car, beloved as it may have been, was just too big, and Phoebe was so small, and maybe she had sneezed or something and lost control, only for a minute, but long enough to make the fatal difference between the ditches and my driveway down the hill.

Or maybe she had just gone off the edge on purpose.

Lacey sighed and looked away. She poured more coffee for Bo, who wasn't taking any pennies for what he thought about the whole thing just then.

She didn't let it go at that—her point made, her opinion aired. She gathered herself up and turned to me, hands on her slim hips, hair tossed prettily back over her shoulders, ready to put an end once and for all to every argument, and pointed out that Phoebe did, after all, have a bumper sticker plastered right there on the back bumper of the car for everyone to see, didn't she? And didn't it read, *Caution!! I Brake for Animals*? As if that were enough evidence for any idiot, even the most feebleminded and blindly loyal of her mother's friends, who would just stop and take the time to think it over. And then she shook her head at me and rolled her eyes back up into their sockets, in perfect parody of the woman that she had so despised.

And what was Lacey doing there in the first place? How come she was around offering up any theories at all about her mother's accident? Phoebe Tooker was dead, but she wasn't in the ground yet when Lacey and John came back home again to Wizen River. And it's my guess that they wouldn't have made the trip even then if it hadn't been for the stranger who showed up one night when Lacey came home to her apartment after work.

No, when Lacey Tooker finally gave in to the boy and agreed to bring him back to the town where he'd been conceived—but not, thanks to Phoebe Tooker's discretion, born—she wasn't, as some of the less alert, but no less talkative, ladies in town supposed, responding to the news that her mother had finally been released from her agonies, both real and imagined, once and for all. Lacey Tooker and her eight-year-old son John didn't travel back east to pay their respects to an old woman that they had loved and would miss.

And she wasn't responding either to what she thought had become his persistent badgering for more information about his mother's hometown.

"Will you listen to this boy?" she said to me when I met them at the bus depot. Her cheeks were pink with embarrassment.

John, after consulting with his schoolmates, all of whom could lay claim to certain men as their fathers, whether those men were actually living in their homes with them or not, insisted that it was his right to at least meet, and Lacey's duty to see to it that he was properly introduced to, the man named Casey Boots who was his dad. Lacey rumpled his hair and laughed and tried to turn it all into a joke by making John the fool there.

Now, those magpies couldn't have known anything at all about John's sudden obsession with finding out the identity of his father. And they wouldn't have guessed, either, about the intruder that Lacey had found hiding in her apartment. But they were all well aware of the mile-wide rift between Lacey and her mother. Gossip is these ladies' business; rumor is their trade. They, all of them, should have figured out first thing that if there was anything at all in this world that had the power to bring Lacey Tooker back home to Wizen River, Nebraska, it wouldn't have been her mother.

Not even her dead mother.

The two women had had their final falling out, after years of unconcealed bickering and mutual harassment, when Lacey was only eighteen. It was then that she had committed the unforgivable and embarrassing crime of getting herself, as they said, "knocked up" during the last semester of her senior year in high school. Not such a misstep anymore. Nobody calls that a crime. Now I'm all the time reading in the magazines about women who get pregnant without being married first. On purpose.

But, for Lacey, it was different. That was before. That was here.

She missed three periods and threw up every morning for a month before her condition was even correctly diagnosed. And her mother, who was at first decently shocked at the news and later cunningly practical about seeing that it was kept a close secret, did what plenty of other women in her position would have done. She sent Lacey west to a home

16

in California to finish her schooling and have her baby there.

And if that Casey Boots had ever had any mind to rectify his wrong by marrying Lacey to legitimate his child, Phoebe and I quickly nipped his good intentions in the bud.

Lacey was too good. She deserved better than that.

The plan was that Lacey would stay in the home until the baby was born. Then she would give the child up for adoption to some more deserving but less fertile woman, regain her pretty figure, and return home to Wizen River with a carefully made-up story about how she had spent the spring and half the summer caring for some sickly second cousin by the beach.

What Phoebe and I, in all our scheming to save Lacey's reputation, never dreamed was that she would change her mind and opt for motherhood after all. All of our plans for her went wrong when Lacey turned pigheaded and maternal on us by refusing to give her baby away.

Phoebe never saw so much as a snapshot of her grandson John. And when the news of Lacey's decision finally hit home and Phoebe had no choice but to accept the fact that Lacey had made up her mind to stay and raise the boy— Jack Tooker had passed on some time before and because he was in the life insurance business at the time, he had left a legacy large enough to make that decision a practicable one—Phoebe wasn't making any secret anymore of the fact that her only daughter had disgraced her by going off and bearing a child out of wedlock. In fact, Lacey later claimed that it was her belief that her mother had actually welcomed the transgression as yet another, and more understandable, cross to bear. The effects of the divorce had lost their impact when Jack Tooker died.

Anyway, it sure wasn't love that brought Lacey and John back to Wizen River for Phoebe's funeral.

It wasn't sorrow, and it wasn't grief.

It was an intruder.

It had to be fear.

* * *

17

The night that Lacey came home from work and found the telegram from me, she also found a man waiting to attack her in her living room. If he had been a little more careful about hiding himself, he might have got away with whatever sick and disgusting entertainments he had in mind for Lacey and himself. Things might have been different. This story might not have been the same.

As it was, she spotted him straight off, before he got the chance to jump her, and she was able to get away.

He made his first mistake when he broke into the apartment and then didn't lock the door up again after himself.

Lacey trusted locked doors. She respected them. Until the killings here began, people in Wizen River had left their doors unlocked as a rule, and so when they did lock them, you could be sure that they meant business.

There were four locks in the front door of Lacey's apartment—the one in the knob and the dead bolt, both of which came with the place, and the sliding bolt and chain latch, which Lacey had installed herself. Lacey had thought that would be enough, and she had taught John, from the time that he was tall enough to reach and old enough to come and go on his own, how to work them all.

And that was why, when Lacey came home from work and found her front door ajar, she straightaway knew that something was wrong. So she didn't, as was her usual habit, lock it all up again after herself once she was inside. If she had, well, things might have turned out very differently for her. And for John, too.

And for all the rest of us, besides.

She was cautious. She called to John, but he didn't answer back. He wasn't there. He hadn't come home from school yet. She went into the living room. She meant to pull back the drapes and take a peek outside to see whether she could spot her son pedaling his way home for supper.

But it was early, and there was still some light outside. Enough, at least, so that the man who had picked his way past Lacey's locks and into her apartment, and who was

18

crouched now behind the drapes, waiting, and who must have considered himself well hidden and all set to pounce on an unsuspecting female or her son, was a shadow in silhouette. If he had been just a little more clever, he would have seen that the light wasn't right for hiding behind anything so flimsy and sheer as draperies, and he would have chosen something more substantial, like an armchair, a sofa, or a closet door.

But, lucky for Lacey, she saw him. She stopped mid-stride, turned on one toe, and made a mad dash for the door.

And if that door had been all locked up, the way it should have been, Lacey would have been trapped. If she had needed to stop and find her keys and fumble with the latches and struggle with the chain, well, there's not much question but that her intruder would have had his way with her.

Anyway, the door wasn't locked. Lacey didn't have to stop. She turned and ran and pulled it open and fled to the safety of a neighboring apartment.

When the woman across the hall, who also happened to be the manager of the building, answered Lacey's knock at the door, she was thrilled to find her usually aloof neighbor framed in the peephole there. It wasn't until Lacey had shoved her aside and made her way to the telephone that the woman realized that this was not a social call.

It was an emergency.

Lacey, to her credit, kept her head. She phoned the police and found a way to give coherent answers to all their questions. Then she pulled back the manager's own draperies and stood at the window to watch for John and, if she could, if her luck held, warn him off.

When he came pedaling up the sidewalk in his usual distracted way—Lacey always worried about him on that bike; he never seemed to be paying the least little bit of attention to what he was doing—she started banging frantically on the glass.

John was so stunned by the sight of his usually calm and sometimes irritatingly rational mother making wild gestures and crazy faces at him from the manager's window, that he rode his bike right up onto the grass, stopped, and toppled over. And there he stayed, staring in amazement, afraid, probably, that the worst had finally happened—that his mother had lost her mind.

Now not only did he not have a father to call his own, but his mother was on her way out, too. He sat right where he had landed in the grass, pinned by his bike and entranced by the unfamiliar sight of her, until the squad cars came.

While Lacey was keeping her son occupied with the spectacle of her gestures in the window, it occurred to her that things could have turned out a whole lot worse than they had so far. What if John had made it home before her that night? Some delay, traffic, or an errand or a talkative coworker, could have kept her later than usual. And John maybe wouldn't have been alert enough to worry about the unlocked door. He might not have noticed the shadow lurking in the drapes.

Lacey suspected that the man to whom that shadow belonged wasn't an ordinary burglar out after somebody's jewelry and cash. She guessed, and she was right, that he probably had something else entirely in mind.

By the time the police found their way to her apartment, the man was long gone. He must have figured that the jig was pretty much up when he heard Lacey leaving. And so the police, who were doing their best to be polite about it, were at first doubtful of Lacey's story. There was no sign of a forced entry. The shadow could have been an illusion dreamed up in the fevered imagination of a paranoid woman. There didn't seem to be anything missing. The television set was still there.

But they changed their minds quickly enough when they came to the bedroom. Someone had definitely been there since Lacey and John had left that morning. Or Lacey was not as normal as she looked.

There were ropes tied to the posts of the bed, and when one officer pulled back the quilt, he found that the mattress was covered with a sickening arrangement of razor blades and knives and matches and wires.

No question about it, that man, whoever he was, had had some kind of violence in mind for Lacey. Whatever he may have lacked in imagination with respect to the hiding place he chose to take, he more than made up for it there.

Lacey hustled John away, out of the room and into the kitchen, trying to cover his eyes and his ears and his whole face all at the same time with her hands, but he wasn't interested anyway. He was still much more concerned about her earlier behavior in the neighbor's window than he was about what the police were finding set up in his mother's bed.

And so that was when the lady from across the hall, having recovered from her shock at Lacey's initial rudeness and the thrill of having policemen on the premises, remembered the telegram that she had signed for earlier that day. She fetched it up from her apartment and brought it to Lacey.

I know what it said, because it was sent to her by me. *Your mother is dead. I'm sorry. Annie D.*

When the police had finished up and gone, Lacey told John that they would be going away. She didn't tell him that his grandmother had been killed. She told the manager that they were off on a little trip and would return in a week or so.

It's quite possible that she really thought that they would.

She phoned the office where she worked and left a message with the answering service there that her mother had died and she would be taking a few days off. It was good that she only had to leave a message, because she didn't want to have to explain, especially not to her supervisor, Richard, who was in love with her and would expect more.

She phoned me in Wizen River to say that she was flying into Omaha and then would take the Greyhound bus from there. And she packed her bags and took off with John for the airport, on her way back home.

The manager of the apartment building where Lacey lived thought that it was the telegram that sent them off. John

21

thought that his mother, after her momentary fit of madness, had finally seen reason and was taking him home to meet his father. And Richard, the supervisor who loved her, thought that she was going back as a way of making some kind of amends for the way that she had treated the poor old woman.

But they were all wrong. Lacey Tooker abandoned her home and her job and her boyfriend in California because she had had a close call with an intruder. In spite of all the locks.

And whatever else she may have felt about Wizen River, Nebraska, she did believe that it was, at least, safe.

3

Up to the Tooker Place

TERRA ES, TERRAM IBIS

The Wizen River runs north and south along the easternmost edge of town, and it forms a natural boundary between the prettier residential areas on one side and the uncleared woods on the other. The streets that run north and east through town lead on out to the farms and fields—Harley Plant's land lay to the east—and the streets that run south lead to the interstate, which is far enough away that not much traffic will take off from it to come into town for food and fuel. The streets that run west lead to the factories.

We have a cereal mill, where all that corn is processed and packaged, and a slaughterhouse, where Jack Tooker worked. The railroad tracks run out that way, too, but the train station where Phoebe and I lent some solace to all those boy-soldiers is now a bus depot, since only freight trains run through here any more. They carry grain and livestock, new cars, chemicals, and toxic waste.

There's a big block of park right downtown in the middle of the business district, and we call it Center Park. It's a pretty place, with a duck pond and a playground, lots of shady oaks and maples, and plenty of benches for the old geezers to loll around on when the weather is warm and fair. We hired Bo to keep Center Park picked up and looking nice, and it's there that the first of our killer's victims was found, too.

She was raped and then strangled right there on the grass next to the playground. It was a real big shock to Rob Murdock, our chief of police, when he found out that a young girl had been murdered not one block away from his office. That was how he decided that it wasn't just some transient who had killed her. It must have been a local boy; no one heard a peep out of the victim.

All the municipal buildings are right there across the street and to the north of Center Park—the firehouse and the city hall and the post office and the jail. Across the street to the east of the park are some shops and the market, and the café that's run by Casey Boots. And then to the west is the grade school. Casey and his sister lived back there behind the school, not too far from the old train station in an area that comes as close as anything in Wizen River to what could be called a slum.

My house, where Dr. Diettermann and I lived and where we raised our boys, is on the other side of town, closer to the river. The Doctor had his office and his examining rooms right there downstairs in our home.

To get to Wizen River from any place farther off than a reasonable car ride, you have to take a plane to Omaha and then catch the Greyhound bus west from there. Lacey had phoned me from the airport and said that they would be in Wizen River in three hours. It was five o'clock in the morning when her call came, and she woke us up. She asked me then how Phoebe had died, and I told her about how the car had been found on its back in the ditch.

It must have been somewhere on the road between Omaha and Wizen River that she came up with the story about the dog in the road.

I had to take Bo with me when I went to get Lacey, because I could not bear to leave him alone and maybe come back later to find him dead. Phoebe had told me that was stupid and silly of me, but . . . well, Bo would have come along anyway.

Never mind how early it was and that his usual habit was to sleep in pretty late. He wanted to see Lacey Tooker. Wild horses would not have kept him away.

He was wearing that old green baseball cap, because it covered up his scars. He had it pulled down over his ears, even though it was a nice warm spring morning. It was May, and all the trees were getting green.

Lacey and her son were standing together on the sidewalk outside when we drove up. They both looked haggard and solemn. John was all puffed up around the eyes from sleeping on the bus. His dark hair was tangled and poked out behind his ears.

Lacey was pale, but she still looked pretty enough. She had her black hair pulled back into a braid, her eyes were as big and blue as her mother's, and as rumpled as she was from the long trip, she still had the same looks that had turned so many boys' heads nine years ago. When she smiled, I was reminded of her dad.

Bo was so excited that he was out of the car and on his way over to greet them even before I had a chance to put the car in park. He ruffled John's snaggled hair like he was some old friend, and when he hugged Lacey, she disappeared within his bulk. She came away laughing.

I heard her tell him that he sure looked, well, great! But that was a lie. It was only her way of being polite. Bo looked terrible, had been looking worse and worse. He had just lost almost twenty pounds, and his cheeks were sucked in, all old and hungry-looking. Lacey wouldn't have known anything else to say but that Bo looked great, even when he didn't.

She stood behind John and sort of pushed him forward with her hands gripping his shoulders—she had pretty, long nails, painted smoky pink—and, looking expectantly at me, she said, "John, this is Annie D."

He smiled sweetly and shook my hand, just like a little

25

gentleman. He said very quietly that he was happy to make my acquaintance. Then he turned back to his mother and said, a little more loudly, "Now can we go see Casey, Mom?"

Lacey wouldn't look at me. The color came back to her face again, all in a pink rush that matched her fingernails, and she turned to Bo and said, "Will you listen to this boy?" She ruffled John's hair and bent over and told him to shut up about Casey Boots right now.

John was a good boy, and he shut right up. He and Bo hefted the bags into the trunk of my car and then John opened the door for Lacey and helped her in. He and Bo climbed into the back seat together, and we drove off across town toward my house.

"Your mother's services are set for this afternoon," I said.

"Good," said Lacey.

"This is a pretty small town, huh, Mom?" asked John.

Lacey turned halfway in her seat to look at him. "Very small," she said.

"I didn't think you'd be here," I went on. "If I'd known, I would have waited, of course. But, well, I went ahead and made the arrangements with the church. Father Philip. And the cemetery. Ward Brothers. You know . . ."

"I remember," Lacey said. She put her hand on my arm. "Thank you, Annie D."

I think that she was just glad that everything had been taken care of and that it would all be over soon.

"It looks empty," John said.

Bo laughed, snorting. To John, even downtown must have been all sky.

"We don't travel much," said Lacey. And then she turned to Bo and asked, "Where's Gunar?"

"I hope you don't mind," I said. "I mean that all the arrangements have been made. There wasn't anybody else to do it, you know. We'll just go back to my house, and you can change there. Get cleaned up. Have a bite to eat. Then

we'll go up to Phoebe's . . . your house . . . later. It wasn't
. . . I'm sorry . . ."

Lacey put her hand on my arm again. "Annie—" she
began.

But Bo interrupted.

"Gunar is gone," he said.

The services for Phoebe were held in the Episcopal church
downtown, the same one that had served the Shireses so
well. Jack and Phoebe had been married there. If Lacey had
married Casey Boots, the ceremony for that rite would have
been performed there. Lacey had been baptized in that
church, and if John had been born in Wizen River, he would
have been christened there, too. It was only fitting that
Phoebe should have had her eulogy read there by the same
old man who had, or would have, performed all those other
services for her.

The casket was kept closed. Phoebe had been so mangled
in the wreck that it was beyond the artistry of the Ward
Brothers to make her presentable again. But that was just as
well, I think. It didn't seem right that John should have had
his first face-to-face meeting with his grandmother when
she was dead. And I doubt that even Lacey much relished
the thought of that sight herself.

Now, it's true that Lacey and her mother did have
their differences. Nobody could ever deny that fact. Each
was as bullheaded as the other when it came to certain
things. They both knew how to take a stand and hold their
ground.

But Lacey was, after all, a mother herself now. And she
must have come to understand some things that had been a
mystery to her once. Like why her mother had gone to such
lengths to protect her. Like why her mother wouldn't let her
settle for what, in the form of Casey Boots, was clearly less
than she deserved. Like why we all kept butting in where
Lacey thought we didn't have any business.

There were some people who said later that Lacey didn't

cry at her own mother's funeral. They said they saw her sit there perfectly composed and cold as ice throughout.

This just isn't true. I saw her crying. I think that Lacey was genuinely sorry that her mother was gone. And I would like to believe that Lacey even felt some little twinges of regret for the fact that they had never been able to bury the hatchet and let bygones be bygones. It was just too bad that everything had gone so far and got so bad that Phoebe and John never met.

John gave his mother his handkerchief. And she used it to cover her face. I saw her shoulders shake. She was crying, I'm sure.

"Aging is the professor of our own death," Father Philip began. He was soft and pink-cheeked, a mild man that the older women, Phoebe among them, who were widowed or divorced or without men for one reason or another, found attractive for his harmlessness and, they thought, his uncanny ability to understand their frustrations and their fears. "Aging teaches us that we are dying every day, not all at once, not in one instant, not at the moment when the last breath leaves our lips, the heart convulses and then stops, or the car flies off the road and crashes into the tree, but bit by bit, day by day, cell by cell by cell. Alas, we are not good students. We are thick and stupid, and slow to learn. The lesson doesn't stick, the message does not sink in, and we find that we have failed that final exam. Not one of us is truly prepared to graduate unto death. We watch others go, and their passing leaves us feeling incomplete, unfinished, and unprepared." He leaned forward in the pulpit, placed his hands flat upon the lectern, and smiled sweetly out over the heads of the friends of Phoebe who had gathered there.

"I'll tell you, I'm not ready," he admitted, laughing, "but make no mistake—it is not because I'm afraid. It's because I want to see the sun rise up over the fields one more time. I've only just begun to understand what the words written in the Bible really mean. I want to see who will win the pennant this year, who will play in the Rose Bowl; I want to go fishing again in the Wizen River. I want to hit a hole-in-one. These are things I have to do! And I need more time!'' He slammed his fist down hard so that one of the ladies in the pew behind us squeaked.

"So, also, was Phoebe Tooker not ready, either.'' He looked down at Lacey and John. "She was taken from us suddenly, and she left many things undone, we know. We're saddened by that. Therein lies the substance of our grief. We're saddened not only because we will miss her. Not only because she is gone and we remain, witnesses to all that she is missing, all that she cannot and will not know. We are saddened because her suddenly taking leave of us is one more unwelcome reminder of our own unfinished business and the deep uncertainties of the time left in our own lives.''

He stopped, and smiled again. Lacey was wringing the handkerchief in her hands like she would kill it, and staring at the floor.

"But pause now, and let this be a moment for happier reflections, too. I want you to indulge in your own good thoughts. Swim in them; let your souls be soothed by the gratitude and the thanksgiving that you feel for this friend and mother that we were fortunate enough to have known. Phoebe Tooker was a good woman, vulnerable and yet at the same time strong. She could be earnest or playful, pensive or glad. She loved her friends, and she carried a special gift for sharing and understanding the feelings of others that made her precious to our lives.''

Lacey coughed into her hand. John swung his feet back and forth.

"Phoebe was a person who cherished her life and all the things in it that were beautiful and rare. I knew Phoebe for many years as her pastor, and we talked many times about faith and obedience, patience and hope. Phoebe was a person who bore a great deal of trial and tribulation in her life, and yet she was able to maintain throughout it all a rich religious faith. She was not ready to leave us and yet at the same time she was prepared for her own death in a deep and necessary way.

"Jesus said, 'Let not your heart be troubled: ye believe in God, believe also in me. In my father's house are many mansions: if it were not so, I would have told you. I go to prepare a place for you.'

"So we must be heartened. For Phoebe so loved God's creation that she gave her life in an effort to spare another. She tried to avoid hitting a dog in the road, and she lost control of her car. She sacrificed her own life so that a poor dog might survive."

He had to have picked that story up from Lacey.

She was holding the hankie to her face and shaking, so I couldn't catch her eye.

"Phoebe Tooker was gentle and kind, unselfish, giving, a neighbor and a friend whose bright light will be sorely missed by the rest of us who were able to comfort ourselves in its warm glow."

Now, if Jack Tooker had been around to hear it, he would probably have taken some exception to the things that Father Philip was saying about Phoebe. But then Jack Tooker's opinion had never held too much water with the rest of us in Wizen River. We didn't care for men of his ilk, too handsome for their own good, men who would leave their wives, walk out after twenty-six years of marriage.

And he was long dead by then anyway. No one was interested anymore in what he had thought of Phoebe Tooker.

"So let us celebrate her life and the new life that she has entered. She has, to use St. Paul's incomparable words, put on immortality. She is gone to us, but is grasped by a presence that is wonderful, that is fulfilling and everlasting and not subject to mortality and death. Let us pray."

Father Philip bowed his head, and the pink flesh of his scalp beneath his thinning hair gleamed.

"Oh God, whose mercies cannot be numbered, accept our prayers on behalf of the soul of thy servant departed, and grant her entrance into the land of light and joy, in the fellowship of thy saints, through Jesus Christ our Lord. Amen.''

We buried her in the Wizen River cemetery with her parents.

Lacey and John both carried away a flower, and I drove them up to the house after it was done.

Four blocks east of Center Park, the main street of Wizen River forks, and one tine of that fork continues on up the bluff through the woods to the Tooker Place. I could see that Lacey was remembering things as we drove up the hill. Bo pointed out the spot where Phoebe had died. There weren't any skid marks on the road—which proved to me that Phoebe hadn't swerved away from any animal—but the bark on that big old oak tree had been skinned clean off one side. The Chevy had been towed away and junked.

The Tooker Place is a wide, two-story house. Back then it was painted white like almost all the other houses in town, except the ones down by the tracks. As if poverty and bad taste go hand in hand, those people paint their shacks all sorts of odd shades. The Bootses' house is peach; maybe the colors brighten up their dismal lives. In winter, when the rest of the world is white with snow, those pastel houses all clustered together look like a child's toy town.

It was to that big house on the hill that Jack Tooker had taken Phoebe after the war. He was working as a foreman in the slaughterhouse then—pork department—and making pretty decent money at it. He said that after all the slaughter he had seen in Europe, he didn't much mind watching all those dumb pigs getting it day after day.

He had wanted very much to settle down after the war. It was as if he had been involved in enough commotion over there to last him for a lifetime, and all he wanted now was to go from day to day, passing the time with sweet, predictable things, like making babies and working to support his family.

Dr. Diettermann was like that, too. They weren't any of them looking for adventures.

31

Jack wanted to fill his big house with children. But then Phoebe lost that first baby, and she had so much trouble carrying and then bearing Lacey that she convinced Dr. Diettermann that she was just grateful to have had one child, and he sent her off to the hospital in Omaha to have a hysterectomy there.

So Jack didn't get what he wanted. Fifteen years later, after the hysterectomy, when his only daughter had grown up into womanhood and Phoebe was beginning to look a little worn to him, he was ready for something altogether new and different. He left his job at the slaughterhouse, went to school nights, and finally set himself up as an insurance agent. He took a look around and figured out that in spite of all his efforts—Jack Tooker dyed his hair to keep the gray from creeping into its rich blackness—he was getting old, just like all the rest of us.

And, so, before it was too late, he said, he packed it up and left his wife.

"I think I got me a big one!!"

Those were Jack Tooker's last words. It was March, 1969, and a second freeze had blustered in and pulled the mercury way down to 10 below. And the wind that day must have taken it on down another fifty degrees at least. But there was Jack Tooker, his dyed hair blowing in the wind, squatted like a madman over a hole in the ice above one of the spots where the Wizen River pools. He was fishing for perch.

It wasn't a perch that he caught, though. A big, old twenty-pound carp took the bait. Jack lost his footing in his efforts to pull it up, and he fell down into his own fishing hole. The current carried him off under the ice, thumping him against the rocks on the bottom and tearing him up on the fallen trees and debris, until finally he snagged on a log near the bridge downtown. Some kids found his body. They were out shoveling the ice off for skating, and what a scare they must have had when they scraped away the snow and found Jack Tooker's bloated face, eyes open, mouth wide with drowning and screaming and terror and pain, staring back at them, his body all broken and torn and swollen and blue and that stupid little fishing pole still held fast in the frozen knot of his fist.

Jack's divorce papers weren't a week old when it happened, and a year later Lacey would leave Wizen River to finish up her pregnancy and have her baby out in California.

But here she was, back with us again. I had to wonder, did it all seem very different to her now? The same trees, some grown taller and more gnarled over the years, still shaded the wide front lawn. The house was more run-down; it needed paint and the gutters were full of leaves. The tire swing that Jack Tooker had fashioned for his little girl when she was young enough to enjoy it still swung from a chain that he had wrapped around the lowest limb of the maple by the garage. The tree had begun to grow around it, burying the chain in its bark.

The extra key that Phoebe had always left out just in case was still hidden on its hook behind the flowerpot on the front porch.

Lacey let us all in, and Bo brought up the bags.

She said, as she stood in the front hall, that nothing had changed.

"It's like a museum," she said, turning. "Time stopped."

There were a few things here and there that must have been unfamiliar to Lacey, but Phoebe's braided rugs still overlapped and covered the hardwood floors, and antique furniture still crowded all the rooms.

"Did she live here all alone?" John asked.

The silence and stillness of the house seemed to echo around us until finally I spoke up and answered him. I said that yes, she did. Without knowing why, I was whispering. Phoebe had rattled around alone in that big house for a long time. She wouldn't listen when I suggested that maybe she ought to sell the thing and buy something more her size downtown.

Lacey kept quiet.

She took John by the hand and led him slowly up the stairs. The wall along the stairwell was cluttered with framed photographs, blurred by a thin sheeting of dust—Jack's parents and grandparents, all grinning, with babies squirming in their arms; Phoebe as a bride, her father, the banker, a pillar at her side; Phoebe's mother in a flower garden, so small and frail she seemed almost transparent; Jack as a soldier standing straight up with his knees locked and his chest out; Lacey as a baby, a dark-haired toddler, a long-legged young girl. We stopped at the landing halfway up to look at the Christmas photo of the three of them grinning beside their tree. That had been the last Christmas that they all spent here together.

The first room on the left at the top of the stairs had been Lacey's. Its windows, with their white eyelet curtains, offered a panoramic view of Wizen River and the land spreading out around it. To Lacey as a little girl, sitting at her window with her dolls, the view must have made all of us look very small indeed.

Across the hall from Lacey's room was what had been her parents' room. There were two twin beds pushed together to make a double covered with a fluffy patchwork comforter that Phoebe had sewn herself. By hand. On the nightstand were all of Phoebe's medications: pills and elixirs and balms. It made the room look like a sickroom, but Phoebe wasn't a true invalid.

Next to Lacey's bedroom was the bathroom. Phoebe's robe still hung on a hook at the back of the door, frazzled gray terry cloth that looked like a dead animal strung up.

At the end of the hallway there were two more bedrooms. One had been Lacey's playroom and was still cluttered with her dolls and toys and books and stuffed animals. The other was Jack's office.

It was all leather and wood. Phoebe had kept it, like

Lacey's playroom, intact. It was as if she thought that in the end her husband and her daughter both would somehow find a way to come back to her.

Lacey walked through the room, picking things up and putting them back down again, until John got restless and went downstairs to explore with Bo. I could hear them calling to each other behind the house.

"This makes me an orphan," she said, turning to me. It was almost as if she were asking me rather than stating the fact of what was true.

"I'll miss your mother," I said. "It's such a shame . . ."

Lacey's eyes glistened. "She was never nice to me."

"No, she didn't mean . . ."

"She liked it when bad things happened."

"No, it wasn't . . ."

"It made her feel useful."

"Lacey . . ."

"I hated her." Lacey stared at me. Tears were rolling down her cheeks, leaving long trails that shone like ice against her skin. She was beautiful. I put out my arms, but she turned away.

"I guess I'll sleep in my old room," she said, wiping her face with the back of her hand. "I don't think I could bear to sleep in hers."

I brought my arms back in and crossed them over my chest, hugging myself instead of Lacey. I told her that I thought whatever arrangement she felt was best would be just fine, and I followed her back downstairs.

The living room was three steps down from the front hall, adjacent to the dining room. And then along another short hallway toward the back of the house was the kitchen. Out the back door was the service porch and steps that led down to the backyard, which spread out to where the woods began again. Phoebe's gardens had all been taken over by weeds.

Lacey stood at the door and called John in. She thanked me and said that she thought she and John could maybe use a little rest. I could see that the day had worn her down.

When I told her that I'd be glad to bring them up some supper, she politely declined my offer. She said she'd like to be alone for a while. She'd call us in the morning.

That was fine. I understood. Bo and I went home then, and on our way down the hill Bo told me that it was sure nice to have Lacey Tooker back around again.

He said that he hadn't felt this good in months.

4

Murder

HORRESCO REFERENS

Sometimes my parents would quarrel. When I was little,
after Weary Shires and his wife had both been buried up on
the slope behind the house, and the farm was all Harley's to
tend to and maintain, and before I was quite old enough to
have become a source of hope and deliverance for my
otherwise hopelessly entrapped mother, they argued about
whether it might really be better after all if we were to move
out, into a more urban setting—my mother mentioned
Omaha, and Lincoln, even South Sioux City, intoning those
words, place names, as if they were magic incantations,
powerful symbols of another world—rather than stay on
like that, in Wizen River, year after year, just scraping by,
with never enough left over for any kind of real luxury.

That was Mona's side of it, anyway. I think that she
figured that if she could only get Harley to come in from the
fields and go back out on the road again, selling whatever
there was to be sold—farm equipment, insurance policies,
real estate, cars—he would remember all about what he had
been missing and might agree to settle down in some place
more metropolitan than Wizen River, Nebraska.

But Harley was not about to budge.

Mona had been the farm girl; she was the one who had grown up there on Weary's land; she had all the history. She even looked like a farmer's wife—not the scrawny, hungry-looking type that Grant Wood made famous, but the hefty kind that you could maybe see on a box of butter, milking cows in a wide, green field. She was long in the arms and legs, big in the chest and through the shoulders, and wide in the waist and hips. She had a body that was meant for hauling hay and bearing children. And yet she was pretty, too. There was an intelligence in her face, a sharpness in her bones that sometimes looked like it might be a challenge or a dare that asked to be crossed and promised no mercy for anyone foolish enough to actually come in and take it up.

She had thick, brown hair that shone red in the right light, and this she tended to herself, lopping if off short, just at her chin and straight around to the back. She pulled it up and away from her face with a big white plastic barrette when she was feeling fancy. Her skin was smooth and pale—she kept it carefully covered and shaded from the sun and never let it brown or burn—and her eyes were green and dark, with just a glint of pale, yellow flame.

It was always my opinion that it had to have been those eyes, so easily driven to maidenly tears, that had touched Harley back in his bookselling days. She dressed herself up in colors that she thought brought out the red in her hair and the green in her eyes, frocks with too much fluff and frill to give any real compliment to her bulk.

Harley was always quick to defend the farm and the town. He truly loved them both. He could go on and on—his voice rumbling up out of some place deep and dark within him, a low, smooth, mesmerizing monotone—about the soil and the trees and the animals and the birds and the seasons sliding in one from the other. And when these panegyrics failed to move Mona, he would fall back on that last bastion, the stronghold in all those arguments, that seems to rise up firm and irrefutable when anyone with a real loyalty to the place tries to turn the head of somebody

38

who has his eye on the lights and bustle of a distant city.

He would reach out for me and pull me into his lap, bounce me a few merry times there on his knee, and say, "Well, but you know now, there's just no place any better in this world for bringing up good-hearted, healthy kids."

And I would grin and bounce and look from one to the other of my parents, hoping that that would be the end of it this time, and my mother would have to finally give in and agree.

She never did, of course. She only humphed at us both and went back to her work, whatever it happened to be just then—she was always busy doing one thing or another, knitting, mending, darning, stitching, hardly ever happy to sit back and take it all in the way that my father so often did. And I would snuggle back down under Harley's arm and look out into the night sky with him, while Mona grumbled and sighed and stabbed that needle in and out of her work as if she meant to do it right to death.

If the Doctor and I had ever argued with each other, and we didn't, it would have been over the way that we were handling the bringing up of our two boys. My own parents had never fought that way over me. Their endless argument was always, beneath its more trivial layers, about whether or not and how soon they would be selling Daniel Shires's house and Weary Shires's land and moving on.

I thought sometimes that the Doctor was just too strict, too set in his ways about what he felt was right and wrong when it came to the way that young boys should behave. He thought that I was too easy, too pliable, too willing to bend and give in to what he saw was fancy and silliness and whim.

"It's a real vorld out dere, Annie, and dose boys got to be ready for it. I should know. Feet on da ground. Heads outa da clouds."

Mona thought that she and Harley and I really ought to be on our way, the sooner the better, before things got any worse for us. Harley wasn't ready to go; he told her and he told me, too, that tomorrow was bound to be a brighter day.

"Give it some time," he said. "Be patient. Wait."

"Carpe diem," Mona would answer, *"quam minimum credula postero."*

The Doctor and I fought small, silent skirmishes, carried out with frowning and sulking until one or the other of us had had enough and was ready to get on with things again. Mona and Harley Plant waged only one long and bitter war, from which Mona was able to ultimately emerge the clear victor.

If the Doctor seemed especially quiet and preoccupied at supper, never quite looking at me and only nodding or pointing a plump finger toward whatever dish he wanted to have passed down the table to his place, it might be because he had overheard me whispering to Bo about how if he planted that stick from his lollipop in a good, fertile place in the garden out back and was sure to water it carefully every day for a whole week, well, then maybe by next Saturday there might have grown up a whole tree of lollipops there, all of them his for the picking.

"Dere vill be no fairy tales in dis house, Annie!" the Doctor had bellowed, slamming the table with his fist.

When the next Saturday came, there was no lollipop tree either, but only the paper stick, limp and shredding from all the water that Bo had been faithfully pouring over it every day that week.

And if the Doctor came upon me sitting and sighing by the fire with my sewing unattended in my lap, he would have to know that I was only worrying over the way that he had scolded Gunar and sent the boy up alone in the dark to his room—where Gunar imagined sly, fierce elephants to be lurking in the shadows—for the way that he'd been talking back to his father out there in the hallway before dinner.

These were only small things, and they were settled and forgiven, and forgotten over time.

But if Mona stormed downstairs in the middle of the night and dumped all of Harley's clean overalls out through the back door into the pouring rain, that was because it was raining again and now he wouldn't be able to finish up the plowing tomorrow either, and if they had been living in a town, and if he had had a respectable, reasonable job, then the rain would only have been an inconvenience and not a disaster. And he would be wearing suits and white shirts and ties instead of those ugly old overalls anyway.

If she picked at him over breakfast about how he had tramped in snow and now it was melting in dirty little puddles on her clean kitchen floor, scrubbed only yesterday, and she still had the red marks on her knees to show for it, that was because what she really wanted was to live someplace where there were sidewalks and someone came out early and cleared away the snow for you before you even went out into it on your way to work.

The sway that Harley had held over Mona by way of the bedroom after that first afternoon when I was conceived and Weary passed his land on to them, never totally lost its power. Still, eventually Mona would come back to her senses and begin to take up arms again against her husband. It started with verbal abuse, which really was harmless enough because he could turn himself deaf as a post by leaning back with the small, infuriatingly satisfied curve to his lips and that blinded look to his eyes, as if he were lost in his own visions of fields that were ripe with corn and barns that were filled with heavy-uddered cows and fat pigs.

He thought that maybe in time Mona couldn't help but come to see just how rich and rewarding farm life could really be if only she would give it half the chance that it demanded and deserved. She only had to open her eyes and her ears and her nostrils and her hands to the rhythms of the earth and its creatures. Then she would see the glory and begin to understand how truly blessed our lives really were, just where we were, doing the things that we were doing.

But Mona had lived there all her life, and she knew what was what.

Harley took her with him down to the barn at sunrise one morning to show her the new litter of piglets that had been born there the night before, with the idea in mind that the sight of their pink and black little bodies might inspire some hope in her. But then three days later the sow had eaten four of her babies and rolled on top of the rest, crushing them, and Mona only shook her head and sucked in her cheeks to say that she had known all along that something like that was bound to happen and it didn't surprise her for one minute when it did.

It never took too much to get Mona started and then to keep her going once she was off. A word about the busted tractor or an ailing hog would be enough to do it. She would warm up with a bit of banging around on her pots and pans and some angry epithets aimed at Harley's ineptitude as a farmer and the futility of his continuing efforts to pursue his profession. And then she would finish it by banging on Harley, too, and he would come away from it all with a black eye or a bloody nose.

I never once saw him hit her back.

He had been brought up to treat a woman like a lady, whether she really was a lady or not, and striking a woman, any woman, even if she was your own wife, even when she had been the one to land the first punch, well, that was one act that ran maddeningly against the grain of all that a man like Harley Plant had been brought up to believe was basic to a man's association with a member of the opposite sex. You don't beat up on babies, and you don't hit your animals, and you never raise your hand against a woman, either. If he had ever gone and let go and unleashed what must have been his own natural violence in defense against his wife, he probably would have ended up killing her.

The first time that I was ever truly a witness to more than just the bruised aftermath of one of those quarrels that finally came to blows was at the supper table on a Sunday afternoon in autumn, just after that first, hard frost had hit and turned whatever had been green to brown and black. We always ate our supper early on Sundays, not because we had spent our morning in church—although Harley often tried to coax Mona into going, reasoning that then at least she could spend some time all dressed up in town. But Mona just wasn't a religious person. Or if she was, then the God that she believed in didn't deserve her worship. He was only some spiteful force that took malicious pleasure in sending bad weather and blight down just to torment her.

We ate early on Sundays because after supper was the time that my mother had set aside for our special studies in Latin and poise.

We must have looked the picture of a loving family come together over a good hot meal that day. It was October, and my mind was on Halloween and what in the world I would be able to come up with to wear for a costume that year. Harley was saying about how we'd be carving the pumpkin to make a jack-o'-lantern for the porch. We'd have to make it scary, he said, with big teeth and mean, slanted eyes.

He had harvested a patch of pumpkins that year for selling on the roadside at a nickel apiece, but since he'd been so busy with other things, what with the tractor broken again, it ended up that Mona and I were doing all the work selling those pumpkins, and she didn't much care for that even though we didn't have all that many buyers, and when we did that was just money in her purse, so maybe she could have been a little bit grateful for that, at least. She found the whole enterprise humiliating, she said. It just wasn't the sort of thing she was interested in doing, standing out in the yard selling pumpkins to the bumpkins.

So when Harley got to the part about carving our jack-o'-lantern, Mona pursed up her lips so tight that they turned hard and white and you could see that she was about to go in and pound on her pots and pans again—they were all battered and worn and dented up from it—and Harley, who saw it coming, but, as always, preferred not to, reached over for the salt cellar as if he didn't have a care in the world past supper. And when he did that, his elbow bumped the gravy boat and it tipped right over and all that greasy brown

43

sauce that Mona had cooked up for pouring over the pork spilled out onto her white lace tablecloth instead.

Mona let out a squeal, at such a high and mouselike pitch that it really was a surprise to hear it coming from the now slack and wide mouth of a person of her proportions, and then she got up from the table so abruptly that her chair, a frail, caned thing that creaked in protest whenever she sat down on it, flipped over behind her with a crack and her thighs knocked the table, jarring it again so that this time the milk in all our glasses trembled and splashed out and soaked into the tablecloth, too.

She threw down her napkin—it floated to the floor next to the broken chair—and moved in one long stride around to Harley's side of the table, and before I even knew what was going on, she pulled back and, holding him almost deli-cately by the chin with one hand, she punched him full in the face with the other. Then she spun out of the dining room and back into the kitchen and was running the water and bashing the pots in the sink.

Harley called that making thunder.

I was so stunned by this performance that I just sat there while Harley, looking baffled, gingerly poked at his nose, which was swelling up red and ugly, and tried to sop up the gravy and the blood with that big blue bandanna that he always kept tucked into the back pocket of his pants.

After that, Mona's occasional assaults on Harley became, along with her much less savage but no less passionate fits of temper, just another part of our regular family routine. There was school every day and our Latin lessons every week, milking every morning and supper every night, and then there were the times when my parents had a fight. Sometimes my mother only pursed her lips and sighed and frowned. Sometimes she stomped off upstairs to bully the furniture, arranging and rearranging dressers and tables and even beds until she had worn herself right out. And sometimes she made thunder.

If weeks went by without an outright attack on my father,

Harley might be thinking that the worst was over now and he could begin to relax again. But I would be expecting something to come along and set her off at any minute, knowing well enough that all of Mona's fury had not been spent, but must be building up higher and stronger, just like a springtime storm. I would be watching for the signs—a drop of sweat on her brow, a pulsing vein in her neck, the hump-hump of her grinding jaw—the same way a weatherman measures the air pressure and tracks the direction of the wind.

And then finally Harley would go and do or say exactly the right thing to rub Mona wrong, and she would, just as I had been expecting, set in on him with a flurry of fists until she felt that her point had been made. After it was all over was when I would take over. I would dash upstairs to fetch the salve and bandages I'd need to patch my pummeled father back up again.

"Well, looks like she's gone and done it again, Annie," Harley would smile and wince while I dabbed on iodine. He kept his hands, which were so big-knuckled and calloused and almost always dirty, especially under the nails, lying there, palms down, on his knees as I tipped back his head to get a better look at the damage that had been done.

"Poor Daddy," I crooned. "Try to keep still."

And Mona would be banging around in the kitchen again or picking a fight with the furniture, dragging it back and forth upstairs. After Harley was cleaned up and bandaged, he would take me with him out to the parlor or the front porch and hold me in his lap and tell me about Chicago or the war or the chickens or whatever it was that he had on his mind, until Mona came out to put me to bed.

Later, I would hear them whispering, Mona whimpering and Harley groaning and the floorboards in their room creaking with the weight and gentle rhythm of their love.

He got to be so good at hushing me up about it all that eventually he just refused to acknowledge what he called his accidents as any kind of beatings at all.

45

When Dr. Diettermann came along and asked me to marry him and I did and we lived in our house in town, before either of my boys was born, the situation back home only got worse for my father. I had hoped that maybe Mona would be content with things now that she could come into town to visit with me and share our success at turning me into a respectable town woman, the wife of the Doctor. But nothing had really changed—she was, after all, still a farm woman, and I guess it's true that her seeing me all set up and settled like that only made her that much more anxious to be off the farm and into town herself.

Harley continued to look badly bruised and battered every time I saw him. Once the Doctor even had to stitch up an ugly gash under his ear. Nevertheless, Harley still wasn't budging, and he still wasn't about to break any of his own rules by hitting her back or even effectively defending himself. He just plain wasn't hearing me when I tried to tell him that he had to do something. He started giving me those excuses whenever it began to look as if I might be thinking of stepping in and trying to do something about the situation.

Or it could be he liked it.

"Aren't I the clumsy one now?" he would say, chuckling as if it were some kind of a joke that just happened to be on him. "But, Annie, I'm telling you," and he would put his hand on my head and lean down to look me in the eye, "you shoulda seen the dent I put into that old door!"

And he would grin and wink and slap his leg and stand up straight again and throw back his head and laugh so hard and deep that pretty soon he had me smiling, too, about the hunk of wood that had met its match when it got in the way of big, old Harley Plant.

Maybe I let him cajole me into accepting his stories for the truth. Once it was that the hog had chased him around the sty and he had had to leap the fence so fast that he caught his boot heel on the top rail and fell right on his face in the mud, and it would have been okay, but, see, there was this rock there in the mud, and wasn't it just like him

46

to go and pick that particular place to hit so his head went smack down on that rock? But I never in my heart doubted that it was anything but Mona's temper that had put all those cuts and bruises there.

So, when Mona finally left, it shouldn't have been too much of a surprise to see how Harley reacted. Still, I knew he loved her, and I expected him to be saddened. I thought that his feelings would be hurt.

"It's just as well, Annie," he said to me. I had come out to the farm to check on them, and he had told me that she was gone. Her closets were empty. She'd left behind only her linens and her pots and pans, her china, and the Latin primer we had shared.

My mother had packed her bags and gone away for good, and Harley Plant was glad.

Myself, I never left Wizen River.

Sometimes I might drive into Lincoln for some special shopping, or to Omaha for Bo, when he needed to see one of the doctors there who treated him, but I never really lived anyplace else. So I don't know for certain whether or not either of my parents was finally right in what they had to say about the place. I did bring up my own two boys here, and they did all right. I think, for a while anyway. And even then, when things began to go wrong for them—for us—I don't think it was because of any bad influence that Wizen River was having on them.

Anyway, that's not the place that I would pick out to put the blame.

A good place to be bringing up kids. You couldn't think of any kind of life that's better. The streets are wide and safe, the fields full of things to see. Friends come from close enough to the same kind of background that parents are able to understand. There's a river to fish in, woods to hunt through. The school's not crowded, and the churches are full.

It only starts to be a problem, really, when the kids get older—too big to be riding bikes and building forts, but not

47

quite ready for a real life of their own yet. I've seen that when the summer heat comes in and school is out for a few months, the young people in town are pretty hard put to find any good, clean fun after dark. There is only one movie theater in town—housed in a building that's at least as old as I am, with tattered curtains and sticky seats and a scratched screen—and one fast-foot hamburger joint, and Casey's, a café where they can come together outside the inhibiting cover of all their parents' good judgment. So, there they'll be, all those good-hearted, healthy kids out looking for some kind of excitement to stir up the air on a muggy summer night.

What they do, then, is congregate in Center Park. What has been a haven for the old folks and a playground for the toddlers by day becomes a nice spot for a little adventure after dark. Even the farm kids—all decked out in their new clothes straight from the more fashionable pages of the Sears or Penney catalogue, and smelling sour with cologne and sweat, their hair combed back with a little spit—will drive their daddies' pickups into town just to hang around for a few hours in Center Park.

Casey Boots and Lacey Tooker had first come together there. Not that they were strangers before that night. There had already been the thing with the dog. But it was really not until they met in the park and went off into the trees that what had been a passing acquaintance, punctuated by one singularly unpleasant incident, began to run a current much deeper and stronger between them.

I don't think that it began in any way that made it very special. Maybe Lacey was with her girlfriends—the nicer girls; surely Neva Jolene wasn't with them—and Casey, Gunar, and Bo were fooling around on the grass nearby, shuffling and laughing too loud, ready to tussle with each other just to relieve their sudden need for physical contact, working up their courage together to find a way to approach those girls. Probably the radios were turned on in the trucks that were parked out on the street. There would have been music, high twanging guitars and heavy throbbing drums.

48

Maybe it was Lacey who, having had it up to there with all that outright shoving that Phoebe had been doing in my boys' direction, latched right on to Casey as the only available alternative. Or maybe he was drawn to her first. She was pretty enough even then. Lacey was never awkward. She turned right from a sweet little girl into an attractive full-grown woman. There never was any in-between time for that one.

They may have talked, Casey and Lacey. She may have said something to make him laugh. Maybe he told her that he would walk her home—Phoebe insisted that her daughter would be the one among her friends to keep respectable hours, even in the summertime when they all of them slept through the mornings as if they had been drugged by the heat—and then maybe they left the knot of other kids and went off together to be alone. Maybe they were holding hands when they walked away; or it could be that Casey waited until they were out of sight before he touched her and tried to kiss her. It happened that way all the time.

And now, so many years later, not much about the whole ritual has changed. The kids are still out there gathering on the green on summer nights, rollicking like rabbits in the moonlight, meeting and flirting, making eyes and holding hands, and sneaking off into the trees to get closer to the one who has been singled out and looks a little special. Maybe the girls are a bit freer with their favors, and the boys more demanding of them in return. I've heard that there is alcohol now and drugs, beer drinking and marijuana smoking, and the music on the radios doesn't seem as pretty or as loving or as sweet. Life all around seems tougher now, and harder and meaner than it used to be.

Everyone's expecting more and somehow turning up with less.

It was there, in Center Park, that the killings started, and it was there on the bench by the duck pond that the first body was found.

Eddie Fly had been one of what my mother liked to call

the bad seeds when I was a girl. He turned up again and again as her example, thrown out to Harley when their quarreling became more desperate and more vicious, too, of what the rigid boundaries of a small town could do to turn a good boy bad. Eddie was only a few years older than I was, and it seemed that trouble followed him no matter where he went, just like the boy in the funny papers with that dark cloud hanging over his head all the time, carrying the rain and thunder and bad news with him from one place to the next.

Except that Eddie Fly made his own trouble for himself. Maybe it was on account of his being such a little piece of a man, shorter and scrawnier than any of the other boys, but wiry, strong, and fast, and that was why it seemed that he was always having to prove his strength, show off his grit and his speed, just in case you didn't know already that a thing was not always to be judged by the size of the package that it came in.

As a youth, he had swaggered through the alleys, smoking cigarettes, one lit against the other, and drinking too much, too often, too soon. He used to say that one day he would be driving a car on TV, but he never did so much more than turn his jalopy over in the ditch out on the straightaway behind the slaughterhouse enough times to make us think that maybe that had finally done some real damage to his brain. Eddie was just a mechanic—at that gas station where Casey Boots went to work that summer after Lacey left town—until his eyes went bad and his hands started to shake and he had to quit. After that, Eddie was a bum.

Eddie Fly had a foul mouth on him, too. One time he gave Phoebe's father, Mr. Wink, a good piece of his dirty little mind, right there in the middle of the sidewalk out in front of the bank, using the worst words and loud enough, too, so everybody would be sure to hear. It was something about the work that he had done on Mr. Wink's car and how Mr. Wink hadn't paid up, even though everybody knew he had more money than anybody else for miles around, and

Mr. Wink said that it hadn't been a good enough piece of work that Eddie did, and he sure wasn't going to pay for it, and Eddie, who took a lot of pride in his skill with a wrench, got mad and started spouting out all those nasty thoughts he had been holding in about Mr. Wink and men like him with all their money and power and all like that. And Mr. Wink, because he was a gentleman, just looked really disgusted, curling his lip as if he had got a whiff of something unpleasant, and then he turned on his heel and walked right off, leaving Eddie Fly there all red and jumping up and down and screaming curses until Mr. Wink had rounded the corner and was out of sight altogether.

The next day there was a big, ugly scratch along the side of Mr. Wink's car just like somebody had taken a screwdriver and dragged it hard and on purpose across the paint. No one could come up with any proof that it had been Eddie Fly, though we had all heard his threats well enough the day before.

Eddie had it in his mind that he was going to save up his money and buy a car that he could fix up himself and take off to the racetrack to drive and make a lot of money winning prizes all around the country until he ended up at the Indy 500 with somebody pouring champagne on his head. He would rather die in a burning car than live forever, he used to say.

But Eddie never was able to get away from Wizen River. He finally had to quit his job at the station, and then he lived alone in his house across the street, getting older and more crotchety, and still making trouble for people all around town.

He was something of a thief. He would pocket things. No one ever did very much to try and stop him, really. He may have spent a few nights in the jail. Ben Franey, who owned the grocery store where Eddie swiped cans of tuna and candy bars on a regular basis, got pretty good at looking the other way whenever Eddie stopped in at his store. Partly that was because Ben figured that there was just no telling what kind of revenge Eddie was going to decide to take against the market, or even Ben Franey himself, if he was ever turned in. And partly it was because he had a soft heart and just felt sorry for the old coot.

Eddie Fly spent his days in the park after he quit working on the cars. You would see him almost every day there, rattling around from dawn to dusk as long as the weather held, pulling faces at the babies and chasing off the stray dogs, walking around with his hands in his pockets, making motor noises—engines revving, gears changing, tires squealing, brakes screaming—with his mouth.

So, it turned out to be Eddy who found the dead girl's body first.

And the shock of it almost did him in. I suppose that he had to bend close to really make out what it was, his eyes were that bad. Probably he touched her. Maybe he nudged her, thinking she was asleep. He laid his head down on her chest, to listen for her heartbeat, to feel her breathing, but there was nothing. She was cold. And dead.

She had been raped, they said. And strangled. The killer—maybe he was just sorry about what had happened; maybe he just couldn't help himself—had done his best to straighten things up after it was all over. Her clothes were piled up nice and tidy under the bench, and she was laid out, with her hands crossed modestly over her breasts. He had even brushed her hair back out of her face. And then he used some scissors and cut away a chunk of it to take home with him as a keepsake. Sort of as a souvenir.

The Wizen River *Gazette*—a thin little rag of a paper with rarely much more than the weather and the hog report printed on its few pages—quoted our police chief, Rob Murdock, guessing that the killer had meant for his victim to be found like that. He hadn't done much to hide his handiwork, Rob said. He was ruling out Eddie Fly as a suspect altogether, because the old man was lying in white shock in a hospital bed, eyes wide open, watching some long race play itself out around a track inside his head.

When he finally came to, a couple of days later, Eddie was full of the story, cussing and swearing, using every horrible, disgusting word in the dictionary to describe what he had seen on the bench in Center Park. They had to keep him inside, locked up and tranquilized, away from the babies and the mothers who had stood gaping, listening to him, in the park.

Her name was Lynette Brady. She was just a perky high school kid who had lived with her family—there were two little brothers, I think—in that purple house next door to the Boots family. She had been in Center Park that night with all the others, and then she and her boyfriend—Jimmy Cline, a tall, thin farmboy who was the hope of the Wizen River High School basketball team—had gone off into the trees together. After trying his best to get her to do what he was asking her to do, and her saying over and over again, "Don't, don't," Jimmy apparently felt that Lynette just wasn't coming across with what he felt he deserved and thought she'd been promising. They had a spat, and Jimmy stomped off in a temper. She must have been on her way home when she met her killer.

Now, although all of us who lived in and around Wizen River were alarmed and frightened when the news came buzzing back about how that girl had been so badly brutalized right there in our park, there really wasn't too much panic until the second victim turned up. Up until then the gossips were saying that it was Jimmy who did it. Some said there were drugs involved. Other people claimed to know for a fact that the girl was pregnant.

But Jimmy Cline was in jail when Nancy Peters died. And she wasn't some trampy teenager in trouble with her boyfriend or her bosses or the law. Nancy Peters was a respectable young mother who was dead.

Her husband had been working the graveyard shift at the slaughterhouse, and he was in bed asleep, and their baby daughter was asleep, too, and Nancy had walked a few blocks into town for some cigarettes and fresh air. She got the cigarettes, all right, and the fresh air, too. When her husband woke up to go to work and heard the baby wailing and no Nancy there for the feeding, he phoned Rob Murdock.

They didn't any of them find Nancy that night, although they did make an effort to look high and low after the husband convinced them that Nancy was not the type of woman who could walk out on her family and not come back. It wasn't until morning that two boys who were out early catching tadpoles in the river stumbled on the body in the grasses by the bridge out back behind my house. Nancy was naked, too, poor thing, laid out with her hands crossed and her clothes all piled up beside her. Raped and strangled and missing a hunk of her hair.

Another keepsake, Rob said. One more souvenir.

There was a picture on the front page of the *Gazette*, of Nancy Peters sitting in a chair by the fireplace, with her baby in her lap and her husband standing up behind her, one hand on her shoulder, a gesture of possession and affection, ownership and love. This had been their Christmas card the year before, the one that she had sent out, with a letter, to their friends.

SECOND WIZEN RIVER VICTIM FOUND was how the headline read. People who were close to Nancy were described as shocked and unbelieving. "She was such a fine person," they said, "friendly. A devoted wife and mother."

"We're following all our leads," Rob Murdock was quoted as saying. He promised that the killer would be caught.

Tom Brady, Lynette's father, a born-again Christian who had started drinking again when his daughter died, stood outside the police station all that day with a sign on a stick that said *Satan Is Here!* and harangued anybody who would listen—out of pity or embarrassment or curiosity or fear—until finally he passed out and Rob Murdock had Lynette's mother come in and take him home.

54

It was then that Lacey Tooker told me her story about the man who had broken into her apartment the day my telegram about what had happened to Phoebe arrived. She'd been in Wizen River for almost two weeks.

Lacey didn't even know Lynette Brady or Nancy Peters, but anyway she was upset. She had the newspaper crumpled up in her hand, and she kept looking out the window for John, calling him inside for no reason, just to see him and to touch him and to be sure that he was fine.

She told me that when she came home from work and found all those queer, nasty things in her bed, all she could think about was John and what if he had come home first, before her? It was that thought and all the sickening images that went with it that had sent her flying back to Nebraska, she said. She said that she had thought that Wizen River would at least be someplace safe.

Safe?

Like I said, the world isn't as nice as it used to be. Or anyway not as sweet as my daddy and I always believed it was. The children who grow up here may be in paradise, but they just don't seem to know that anymore. They've got their eyes on the shopping malls and the record stores. They walk around in T-shirts with skeletons and bodies and bloody knives printed on the back. They die in their beds; they drown in the rivers; they kill each other in their cars. They sit inside at night now, glued to their television sets. Every place is dangerous, is what they learn. Not one place is really safe. The whole wide world could be blown up into smithereens any single day.

By now almost all of us here have begun to lock our doors.

5

The Port-Wine Stain

VULTUS EST INDEX ANIMI

When I was still a schoolgirl, there was in town an older woman named Nellie Grace Simpson who lived in that bitty white house on Center Street, up by the hill, and what she lacked for luxury in her home was more than made up for on the grounds. She had the most plush and pretty lawn and gardens in all of Wizen River. When that smoking, rattling yellow hulk of a bus brought all of us farm kids in from the fields for school, its route went right down Center Street, and through the smudgy window I could, when the weather was fine, see Miss Simpson out there in her yard waging her war against the dandelions and the weeds.

She wore baggy overalls rolled up too high, thin white ankle socks pulled up over her dappled shins, heavy sensible shoes that would suck those socks down into their heels, and a broad-brimmed straw hat set squarely on her head to keep the sun from shining too fiercely in her face.

Some of the more mischievous boys—and I'm sure Jack Tooker was one of them—used to take great delight in tormenting poor old Nellie Grace. Sometimes they would get a stray pup and send him across the grass to lift his leg against that fir tree that she had growing there to hide her front window from the peering eyes of any nosy neighbor.

They would stand out in the street with the unsuspecting mutt that they'd collared and then push him up into the yard, all shouting, "Go on, dog, go pee on Nellie's tree!"

And although the dog hardly ever complied with their wishes, just the noise of their chorus was enough to bring that old woman storming out the door and down the front steps, waving a broom as if she were fighting off some horde of nasty rats rather than a crowd of rowdy boys. When they got older and braver, and meaner, too, they drove their cars across the grass and left muddy tire tracks in her lawn.

Nellie Grace Simpson's gardens were truly a sight to be admired. She had flowers of every color and kind coming up in tiers along the brick paths out back, and grass that stretched out clean and green and carefully clipped all the way from her doorstep to the curb. In the wintertime, when Nebraska turned cold and the ground froze and the snow settled in, she took her green plants and potted flowers into the house. Her windows were always fogged over with what I liked to think of as plant breath.

Then, when Nellie Grace Simpson died, her heirs—two witless little nieces in long coats and high heels—sold the property, and the men came in with their big machines and razed the house and bulldozed the flowerbeds and built a big supermarket there on the lot.

Miss Simpson was truly an inspiration to me. I knew from the time that I was old enough to notice Mona's fidgeting that my mother had big plans for me, and that if she had her way, I wouldn't always be hanging around Harley's farm, where growing things was not a hobby, but a business. And so, many years before Dr. Diettermann came to town to grant all of my mother's wishes for me, I had determined that when I was married and living in a house, my gardens would flourish under my care just the same way that Miss Simpson's had under hers.

When Germany lost a war and a physician to the more

peaceful folks of Wizen River, and he changed my name from Annie Plant to Annie D., and I left Mona and Harley to live like a lady in town, I had a yard and gardens to call my own, and I kept that promise to myself by cultivating them in a way that would have made my mentor proud.

Bo said that he thought of mine as a magic touch. He said it could bring to life and nurture plants and flowers and children, and even men, by which I guessed he meant his father.

Of course, there always was much more to it than just a touch.

Mona and Harley, when they drove into town on a Sunday afternoon to visit with me and my Doctor in that short year before Gunar was born and Mona was gone, would always take the time to survey the flowerbeds out back. And although my father's praise and admiration were sincere and his advice well considered, Mona's shrill exclamations were always given with an eye to please the Doctor. I know how it rankled her to take my hand and feel the calluses that had grown against the rough handle of my spade or spy the dirt that had settled there beneath my neglected nails.

And the Doctor, well, he would slap me on the bottom, as if I were some hefty hausfrau and say, "Ach, meine Frau, Annie, if you are happy, den happy, too, I vill be, okay!"

That first year, when he was still struggling to gain his patients' confidence and I was getting myself accustomed to the novelty of being a matron with a house of my own in town, and Gunar was growing there in my belly, making everything difficult and more promising at the same time, the Doctor pampered me and cared for me, and I grew fond of him in return. I didn't think of it as love, really, until those few ecstatic moments just after Gunar was born.

The Doctor, though he had a booming voice and commanding manner, was not a large man. In fact, he was short. Not small, exactly. But compact, as if all the brawn and muscle

58

of a man like Harley had been pushed down and out to make a rounder, squatter form. He had bright blue eyes that crinkled up and all but disappeared when he laughed, which was often enough. He parted his hair in the center of his head and then combed it flat back behind his ears so that it looked more like a tight-fitting cap than a head of hair on his round skull. It always hung a bit too long in the back and tended to separate into greasy strands against the starched white collar of his coat.

When Dr. Diettermann looked in the mirror, he never did see himself from behind.

His patients would begin to arrive at our door around nine o'clock—mothers with cranky babies, children with noisy coughs or bloody noses, old men with unreliable hearts, farmers with missing fingers, and young women heavy with child.

He had a nurse, Darla Williams, who worked for him for many, many years. She was a serious, frowning woman with dark, wavy hair and very pale skin and a mole, a beauty mark, really, on her chin, just under her lip, so perfectly round that it looked as if she could have painted it there with an eyebrow pencil.

While the Doctor and Darla were seeing to the patients' various complaints in the examining room off the parlor, I would be outside in the sun, tending to my flowers. Then, at noon, Darla took off for lunch, the patients all went home, cured or eased or at least reassured, and the Doctor and I sat down together at the old oak table in the kitchen to share our meal.

"Poor Mrs. Anderson," I remember him saying to me one day as we ate. "Not good feet on dat vun." He shook his head and pulled his napkin down into his lap. "In Germany, Annie, ve vould send her to a spa."

"A spa?"

"Ja. Healing vaters. My own Uncle Gunar . . ."

That was the uncle after whom we would name our first son. He and Jan were brothers whose pranks were a source of constant embarrassment to their prim sister, the Doctor's

59

mother, and a delight to the Doctor as a boy. There was a younger sister, too, Else, who by all description was fair and innocent and perfect.

The Doctor dabbed his lips with his napkin—leaving a crumb stuck to his chin that worried and annoyed me until I couldn't stand it anymore and I had to reach over and pick it off myself—and he laughed and shook his head.

"Ah, Annie," he said, "if only you could have seen my poor sveet mother's face ven dose two come in all covered in mud like dat and carrying Else and me, just as filthy, under deir arms like two squealing . . . vas is das? Piggies!"

He was able to put away his memories as completely as he had put away his lunch, going back to his work and the people who needed him.

It wasn't until after dark, when supper was done and the rest of Wizen River had put their troubles away with the dishes and gone to sleep, that all that good cheer retired, too, and the Doctor's happy reminiscences gave way to nightmare and grief. Then, in the moonlight that sneaked in through the curtains at our bedroom window and fell down on him like an icy white blanket, those apple cheeks sagged and his bright eyes hardened, turned cold, furtive, and piglike in their folds of flesh. And those plump little hands that had all day long been so precise in probing and soothing the bodies of his patients, shook as they carried one cigarette after another up to his tight, white lips.

Just as the Doctor never saw the back of his own head in the glass, so no one but me was ever treated to so much as a glimpse of this, his darker side.

To his patients he could be efficient and professional, compassionate or cool. Darla Williams was devoted to him. Phoebe Tooker came to depend on and adore him. To my parents he was always courteous and contained. Even Harley came to tolerate him. And to our boys he was both gentle and firm.

*   *   *

My mother never saw my sons, her grandchildren. She could have if she had only had the patience, or the inclination, to push her famous getaway back a few months. Mona took off on her own, never to be seen again, and three months later, in January 1950, Darla and the Doctor and I delivered Gunar Diettermann upstairs in my bed.

It was one of the coldest winters ever to settle down on Wizen River, and Phoebe Tooker had come down the hill to visit. We were in the kitchen, and I had put out coffee and cake to take away the chill.

I was sitting there on the stepstool by the stove, moaning to Phoebe about all the difficulties a pregnant woman has to contend with, when my baby rolled and kicked. My body was shaken by an odd rumble, deep inside. Before I could set my cup straight in its saucer, there was bloody brown water running down my legs and pooling on the linoleum at my feet.

Phoebe went wild with panic. I don't know what she must have thought had happened. She plowed past me, out of the kitchen and through the house, screaming for Darla and the Doctor to come quick.

I was down on my hands and knees in the kitchen, trying to sop up my puddle with a tea towel, when Darla came in and the first contraction gripped me. When the pain subsided and I took the time to look up, I could see that Phoebe was wringing her hands and rolling her eyes at me.

Together she and Darla helped me struggle to my feet and started to take me up to my bed. Somewhere between the kitchen and the stairs, though, Phoebe decided that she had had enough. She let go of my arm and disappeared—gone, I'm sure, to spread the news of Gunar's impending arrival. All I could do was apologize for the mess that I had made in the kitchen and plead with Darla to please let me just clean it up now before it made a stain.

She went ahead and undressed me, dumping my dampened skirt into the hamper with the Doctor's own laundry, as if there were no difference between its filth and the dirt in his socks, and then she nestled me down into the bed. She went back downstairs to the parlor to get the Doctor and send the patients who had been waiting for him home. They must have been annoyed, having trekked out into the cold like that only to be turned away again.

When I cried out, Darla shushed me. When I thought that I couldn't bear it anymore, the Doctor urged me on, and when it came time to push, they smiled and told me I was doing just fine.

"Schiebe, Annie! Schiebe! Schiebe!" he cried.

And so I stared into the black well of Darla Williams's beauty mark, and I did what the Doctor said. I pushed, and I didn't want to do anything wrong, and I pushed, and I tried not to make too much noise, and I pushed some more, and finally Gunar Shires Diettermann was born.

There the Doctor was, his flat black cap of hair mussed and fallen into his face, his cheeks all puffed up and flushed rosy, and his bright blue eyes here again and gone again in the crinkles of his smiles.

And there was Gunar, wet and red and pinched up like a monkey, squalling in the Doctor's hands. He laid the baby on my breast, and that quieted Gunar some, and then the Doctor got all grim again as he put his fat sausage hands on my belly and began to knead. If it hadn't been for Gunar lying there so precariously in my arms, I would have struck out at the Doctor for hurting me then, like that, just when everything was beginning to be so perfect. But then the placenta was passed and the cord was cut, and all I could think of was the mess, the mess.

Four years later, in 1954, we did it all over again with Bo, but then it was summertime and I was alone out in the garden when my water broke, and that was better because there wasn't so much mess. And I knew that it was very good for my flowers. The ones in that particular spot always seemed to me to turn out bigger and stronger, more brightly colored, too.

*   *   *

At about the same time that Bo was born, that summer when it was so hot and there had been no rain and the farmers were beginning to fret over the dwarfish corn and yellowing soybeans, Casey Boots's poor mother was as big as a barn with her second baby. Once again the Doctor was seeing to it that she took proper care of herself.

I've always called her "poor Mrs. Boots," because that's exactly what she was. I felt sorry for her, partly because she had always been poor and partly because her irresponsible rake of a husband had packed up and left her, but mostly because she was just the kind of woman who never seems to have any luck at all.

For a while.

She might have thought herself better off to be rid of that no-good man of hers. I'm sure he must have beat her, and Casey, too. And she could have counted it her good fortune as well to have been the one who got the job as our housekeeper several weeks later, after the baby was born. I know that she truly believed that all her years of struggle and need had finally paid her back in full when she and Casey and her grandson John ended up living there on the hill with the Tooker Place to call their own.

But back then, before Lacey Tooker began to figure into things, when Gunar was four and Casey was just a tot of two and his little sister was still only a bulge in his mother's belly, and there was no husband to be going out and bringing home a paycheck to buy food for the three of them, I just couldn't help but feel a little sorry for her.

She was proud enough to be embarrassed by my sympathy.

Mrs. Boots was, when not all bloated up with her babies, a tall, thin bag of bones, draped in dresses that she made for herself, assembling them from old patterns that had served her better when she was still young and plump.

She and Casey would set off on a walk across town to our house for her appointment with the Doctor. And that summer, if I was in the yard with Gunar beside me in the dirt and Bo bundled up asleep in his basket in the shade, she would stop to admire my flowers and my boys.

"Annie D.," she would smile and say, "you have such a nice garden."

The name had caught on and stuck even with the people who knew me the least.

"I can't imagine how you find the time to do it," she said.

"Oh, it doesn't take much . . ."

She'd shake her head and laugh. "But you must be so busy. With those two boys. And your husband. And your house." Hands on her hips, knees locked, feet spread, belly up and out, she'd purse up her lips and shake her head. "Can't imagine," she would say. "No idea how."

Casey was such a pretty little boy back then, with dark curls that were always too long and too thick and spilled down into his eyes so that you only saw the terror there when he reached up to brush them away and take a peek around to make sure that there wasn't anything hiding just out of sight behind him.

He would plop down onto the lawn to watch us while his mother went inside for her examination. When she came back out again, if Casey was crying or if Gunar was crying, and sometimes even if Bo was crying, Mrs. Boots would haul her boy up to his feet and slap him hard on the face and apologize to me for what she assumed must have been his mischief.

It was a nice sunny day, not too hot, and Mrs. Boots had come with Casey and left him in the yard with me, and he was sitting quietly on the grass there watching me prune my roses, and I asked him what he thought about the fact that pretty soon he was going to be a big brother, just like Gunar.

I expected him to puff up with some of Gunar's swagger and tell me just how he was feeling, but that isn't what Casey did. He took a quick look over his shoulder to be sure that there wasn't anybody or anything there, and then he put his small face in his hands, and he started to cry. I was so afraid that his mother would come back into the yard just

64

then and see him crying and slap him for causing me trouble that I took off my gloves and sat down and pulled him over into my lap there in the grass. He held on to me with a desperation that I had never felt before in anyone so small, and when I finally had him hushed and sucking on his thumb, I ventured further, risking more tears, and asked him what was wrong.

He told me that it was a monster, and that it was going to get him.

I hid my smile and brushed his hair back from his face and started to tell him all the reassuring things that I had explained to Gunar—that there are no monsters and that elephants are too big to fit in your closet or under your bed. But Casey only sucked that much harder on his thumb and shook his head so that the curls slipped back down over his eyes.

"Monster," he said.

"Where?" I asked, peering at him through that curtain of hair and swinging my hand out wide in a sweep that was meant to include the gardens and the house and Wizen River and even all of Nebraska in its arc. "Where is there a monster, Casey?"

But before the boy had time to answer me, his mother came into view, trudging down the garden path with her big belly leading the way. She was smiling, glad, I think, to see that Casey was quiet and Bo was still napping peacefully and Gunar, though dirty, was amusing himself very well with the innards of an unlucky worm, and none of them seemed to be making any bother for me.

She knelt down next to her son and wove her bony fingers in through his curls. She gave me the happy news that the Doctor had told her that the baby had dropped and it wouldn't be very much longer now. I suppose that was good because she was planning to get a job somewhere, and bring in a little cash to add a few extra inches to the shoestring that she and Casey had been getting by on in the impoverished months since Mr. Boots had walked.

Then little Casey, who had been studying the landscape,

65

still searching for an answer to my question and at the same time making absolutely sure that I was right and there really were no fiends hidden in the flowers, jumped up and cried, "There! Monster there!" and ran off down the path, deeper into the garden, leaving some of his hair still knotted in his mother's hand.

He had pointed at her.

Well, not at her exactly. More at her big belly.

Mrs. Boots looked after her son, who had disappeared into the foliage, and then at her fingers, which were tangled with his dark hair, and then at her belly, which was full of her baby, and then at me.

"He thinks," she said, frowning and shaking the hair out of her hand, "that I have a monster in my tummy." She looked again to where Casey had run, but he was hiding.

"It's his age," I said. "That age. Gunar used to—"

She smiled at me. "I'm sure," she said, before I could finish. "Of course." She grinned at Gunar and shrugged. "Excuse me," she said.

She walked off to fetch her son out of the bushes.

I heard the slap and Casey's cry, which softened down to a whimper as they passed through the gate to the street.

So that was what it was. Casey's mind had conjured up a beast and then planted it deep inside his mother, a safe enough place for a while, until it began to grow and kept getting bigger and now was threatening to be born.

Two weeks later, on a Sunday evening, just as we were all sitting down to supper, the telephone rang, and it was Mrs. Boots calling to say that the time had come and the baby was on its way and everything was fine so far.

Except that Casey was hysterical.

The Doctor told her that he would be there, hung up the phone, came back to the table, and told me just what Mrs. Boots had said to him. And how was he supposed to deliver a baby, he wanted to know, with that Boots boy screaming two-year-old terror in the next room?

Although he was truly devoted to his work and to his

patients, I know that there were times when the Doctor really wished that he had been able to find a bigger town to settle in, one with a hospital at least, where babies could be born and old men could die without all the neighbors out on their porches, listening in.

I told him that I'd go along. It was the least I could do. I'd bring Casey back home to spend the night with us. We called a neighbor girl to come in and keep watch over our own two boys, and the Doctor gathered up his equipment and we drove across town to the Bootses' house, which was really not much more than a peach-colored shack, full of icy drafts in winter and a pocket of breathless heat in summer.

Mrs. Boots was inside, lying on the ratty sofa with her knees pulled up, fighting off the pain of each successive contraction. And Casey was in the kitchen huddled up under the table in the corner, battling his own pain by banging his head against the table leg.

I strode into the kitchen, yanked him out from under there, threw him over my shoulder, and carried him out, leaving the Doctor and his patient to their work.

Casey calmed down as soon as we were in the car. Probably he thought that I was going to take him home and keep him there, safe from all the monsters in his own family. When we got back to the house, I carried him upstairs, more gently now, put him into a pair of Gunar's pajamas, and tucked him into the extra bed in Bo's room. I left him lying there with his thumb in his mouth and his eyes wide open, staring at the ceiling in the dark.

The Doctor came in many hours later. It was a warm, clear night. Mrs. Boots and her newborn daughter were doing just fine. She had named the baby Neva Jolene.

Sometime before dawn Casey came creeping into our room, and he woke me with his soft touch. I pulled him into the bed with me and cuddled him up close.

"Casey, honey," I whispered. "You have a little sister. Isn't that good news? Isn't that nice?"

He just stared at me with his wide blue eyes.

"Your mamma's fine," I said.

Casey reached out and put his small hand on my face. "No monster?" he whispered.

"No monster."

He smiled at me.

"A baby," I said. "Your sister. And your mamma's named her Neva Jolene."

"No monster," he said again.

"No monster." I pushed his hair back from his face, and he nuzzled against my hand.

On the other side of the bed, the Doctor kicked and moaned.

I had to take Casey back to his mother again in the morning. I would have liked to stop and get his curls trimmed by the barber on our way across town, but that wasn't my place.

When we walked into the house, through the half-hinged screen door that wasn't barrier enough against the flies, there was Mrs. Boots, still on the sofa, but more serene now, her newborn baby swaddled up in a blanket and sleeping peacefully in her arms. Casey gave me a pleading look and tried to scoot back between my legs and out the door, but I caught him and nudged him on, closer, to get a good peek at her.

Little Casey Boots's worst fears were realized then.

Neva Jolene was a baby all right. And she wasn't a monster. But to Casey she might just as well have been.

Mrs. Boots had, in spite of the heat, wrapped the baby's tiny body so closely into the blanket that only her face was visible. Casey responded to my prodding and moved forward, closer, until he was right up next to the sofa. Then he bent over, with his curls brushing the baby's face, and he took one look, let out a howl, and ran back past me to his old spot under the kitchen table.

Mrs. Boots swung one hand over her head and out to nab him with a slap before he got away, but he was too quick for her, and her hand fell short and caught me on the hip instead. That jostled the baby, who had already been stirred by Casey's reaction, and she began to wail. Mrs. Boots began to apologize to me for the blow that had been meant for her son, and I stepped in just a little closer to get a peek at the baby for myself.

Now the Doctor had come in very late the night before, and I had been asleep and was maybe a little groggy, that much was true. But I did remember him coming in, and I did remember his telling me that Mrs. Boots had had a baby girl and that her name was Neva Jolene. I didn't remember his saying anything else about it.

He just hadn't told me.

But there it was.

A birthmark, a port-wine stain, that splotched the left side of Neva Jolene's small face from her neck right on up to just below her eye and got redder and fiercer as she bawled.

Mrs. Boots slipped her nightie down over her shoulder, pulled out one of her swollen breasts, and fitted the nipple into Neva Jolene's mouth.

Then she smiled and said, "Well, she's pretty enough from this side, isn't she?"

And she was. With the stained cheek pressed close and hidden against her mother, she was an ordinary, even pretty, baby, sucking happily. And I nodded and smiled and offered my congratulations and best wishes and all of that.

And then I left. There really wasn't anything more for me to do. The neighbor ladies would be coming in to help.

I heard Casey's whimper and the thud of his head against the table leg as I was leaving, but it didn't really seem right for me to interfere. It wasn't any of my business, after all.

Mrs. Boots said, "Don't worry, Annie D. We'll be fine. You'll see. Casey'll get used to this. He'll have to."

Then the screen door slapped shut behind me, and I went home.

6

Blue's Been Killed

DUX FEMINA FACTI

When Gunar was three, I gashed his little finger, right down
to the bone, with one of the Doctor's razor-sharp scalpels.
It was an accident. And when Bo was two, I knocked him
down, and he fell and cut his forehead open, right between
the eyes, on the edge of the coffee table in the living room.
That was an accident, too.

I was only trying to get the scalpel away from Gunar
before he sliced himself or his brother with it, and when he
turned it into a game of keep-away, I got angry and grabbed
and pulled, and as I pulled, the blade caught his finger,
because he was stubborn and wouldn't let go, and cut right
into it. Almost to the bone.

I won't forget the ache that slammed like a fist into my
stomach when I felt that blade slipping down along the flesh
of his small finger.

And Bo had been running wild around the living room, and
I saw that he might fall, so I tried to stop him, or at least
to slow him down, but he wouldn't listen to me. When I
caught hold of his legs, he did fall, and when he fell, his
head flopped forward and down against the table edge.

There was so much blood. Head wounds are like that, the Doctor said.

He sewed Gunar's finger back together with seven stitches; it took ten to mend Bo. And the Doctor told me that all my precaution was causing more accidents than it was preventing.

"Back avay, Annie," he said. "You sometimes are too much too close."

Maybe I did lean just a little bit on this side of being overprotective of my boys. But if I did, it was because it was a natural thing to do, and I couldn't help myself. There were so many ways for them to be hurt, and I was always imagining the very worst. If Gunar had the hammer and was peacefully pounding nails into a chunk of wood that the Doctor had given him, I watched and worried that Bo might provoke Gunar into bashing him. And if the boys were out back at the swing and Gunar was pushing Bo higher and higher, I was afraid that Bo might forget and let go and fall and break his neck or his back or his head or something worse than that. Or that Gunar might look away and the swing might hit him and knock him to the ground.

Nothing ever really happened.

It was just that they both always seemed to me to be so small and so helpless, even when they got bigger and more independent, that it amazed and terrified me sometimes to think that their safety and their well-being and their lives even, were in my hands, at the mercy of my capabilities, dependent almost totally upon nobody but me. And the Doctor. I wanted them to be sure, especially since I wasn't ever, quite, that I was reliable.

I even went so far as to hang up photos of myself and the Doctor, in serene, peaceful, happy poses that I thought looked reassuring, on the wall in each of the boys' rooms, up above the foot of the bed where they could see them. I thought then that they would feel more secure knowing that their mom and dad were always close by to keep and care for them, and that they could take some comfort, if they happened to wake up in the middle of the night with ideas of elephants thundering in the closet—that was Gunar—or salamanders squirming on the floor—Bo—to see in the glow of the nightlight the smiling faces of myself and the Doctor gazing sweetly down upon them.

It seemed like such a good idea at the time; years later I learned from Gunar that those pictures had always made him feel that he was being watched.

Sometimes when it was late, after I had put them to bed and gone to bed myself and then got up again when the Doctor cried out in one of his dreams and took to his chair by the window, I would creep quietly into their rooms just to look in on my boys, who always seemed even more vulnerable when they were asleep like that. Gunar would be all sprawled out on his bed, with his bare feet poking out from under the warmth of the covers and the pillow over his head, and Bo would be curled up into a tight little ball, just a hump beneath the blanket on his bed. And I thought then that I could bear anything at all in this world except if it was to be that I should have to see one of my sons suffer.

At least I could say that there was nothing in the world the matter with my boys back then. Not like that Neva Jolene Boots, with her face all splotched up red on one side, and her brother, pretty enough with his blue eyes and his curls, but afraid of every little thing and always banging his head against the furniture when anybody crossed him or he didn't get his way.

I didn't see those children again after Neva Jolene was born until Mrs. Boots brought them in with her when she came to see the Doctor for her six-week check.

It was finally raining again and had been all week, which pleased the farmers well enough until it began to look like the fields would flood if it didn't let up soon. I was going nearly crazy cooped up inside with Bo cutting his first teeth and Gunar throwing a tantrum over the slightest challenge to his will. I was standing at the upstairs window, looking out at the rain and sighing and straining to come up with some fun project to keep Gunar and myself occupied and amused, when I spotted Mrs. Boots trudging up the street toward our house.

Her head was bent forward under the broad brim of her flowered vinyl hat, but I could see that she was biting down hard and puckering her lips in a kiss of determination. Her big, bony body was draped in a wide, yellow poncho that was way too large and hung down and dragged along through the puddles behind her like a slick bridal train. She was carrying Neva Jolene in her arms, and if I hadn't known better, I might have thought, looking at her and the way that baby humped out under the poncho, that she was still heavy with child.

On her feet she wore black buckled galoshes that her husband must have left behind, and with every step she took one or the other of them stomped down and splashed up rainwater all over Casey. He was hurrying along beside her, desperate to keep up, carrying a torn black umbrella, but not quite skillfully enough. He would lose his balance and let it tip forward, and then the rain came splashing down on his bare head without any mercy at all.

They must have walked like that the whole long way across town.

I hurried downstairs to help them into the house, and just as I opened the door, a crack of thunder sent Casey bolting in sheer terror. He bumped smack into me and almost knocked me flat, and if I hadn't laughed and caught my balance in time, Mrs. Boots would have shown him the back of her hand for sure.

Casey was drenched. So I took him and Neva Jolene, too, back to the kitchen with me, deaf to all of Mrs. Boots's protests and apologies and shy gratitude. I stripped Casey bare and put him into some dry, clean clothes of Gunar's and toweled his hair and combed it back away from his eyes. We were just sitting down at the table to eat some cookies and color some pictures when Mrs. Boots returned.

Neva Jolene was asleep in Bo's basket, and Bo was in his highchair chewing on some toast, and Gunar and Casey and I were sorting through the crayons—looking for green

because that was the color Gunar always liked the best—
and no one was making any trouble. That pleased Mrs.
Boots and was a great relief to me. But instead of gathering
her children up to make her way back home again, she set
her bag down on a chair, pushed the sleeves of her sweater
up past her elbows, and began to wash the breakfast dishes
that I had left piled up dirty and soaking in my sink.

"You know, Annie D.," she said to me over her
shoulder and out of the side of her mouth, "what you need
around here is some help. You know, somebody who could
come in and do some of this work here so's you could have
all the time you need to spend with your boys. And your
flowers."

She was standing at the sink, and the window there looks
out onto the garden, so she stopped for just a minute and
gazed out as if to stress the sincerity of her idea to me. Then
she went back to her scrubbing and I went back to my
coloring and she kept right on talking, explaining the
situation that she had in mind.

"See, I could come in here, say, every other day. Not
every day, you know, 'cause of course I do have my own
kids and my own house and all to mind. Not so much as all
of this, is what, and so, you understand, I got the time. All
the time I need, anyway. I could take care of some of this
work here for you so's you could have some of that time,
too. You know, to spend."

And outside it was raining cats and dogs and inside the
kitchen it was warm and cozy, and there I was coloring
inside the lines, in green, with Gunar and Casey, and there
was that bony Mrs. Boots standing at my sink washing up
the dishes, still in her black galoshes, going on and on about
how she had this friend next door, in that orange house, you
know, the one with the fence, who said only this morning
how she'd watch the Boots kids for nothing, or next to
nothing anyway. Now that Mr. Boots was gone—and here
she stopped scrubbing again and turned to give me a squinty
look over her shoulder that I think was supposed to be some
kind of a warning to me that I should keep on my toes in

74

pleasing the Doctor or I might find out that I was standing in Mrs. Boots's galoshes myself one day—with Mr. Boots gone, she really needed the money, just the same way I needed the time.

You know, to spend.

And she kept going on and on, washing and drying and wiping up, and by the time that she was finished and had ducked into her poncho again, I had hired her as my housekeeper to come in three days a week to do whatever it was that needed to be done. And then she gathered up her kids, said she'd see me again in the morning, and went back out into the rain and home.

It never felt exactly right to me that I should have in my employ a woman who was my age, and had two children who were my children's ages and needed the same looking after as my children did. But, then, Dr. Diettermann had not run off and left me the way her husband had.

Sometimes she brought Casey and Neva Jolene over to the house with her, and I would look after the children while she did the cleaning, and that got rid of my guilt all right, I guess, and only became a real problem when those three boys grew bigger and kept ganging up together against that ugly little Neva Jolene.

Anyway, that was how it came about that Gunar and Bo were such good friends with that Casey Boots and still hung around with him later when they all were off to school.

Wizen River is a small enough town, it's true, and most everybody knows most everybody else here, at least by name and occupation if not any better than that, and Bo and Gunar would probably have been acquainted with Casey and Neva Jolene Boots no matter what the circumstances were at home. But because their mother worked for us and wanted something a little bit better for them, and because they had all of them been coming around to our house ever since Neva Jolene was just a bitty newborn, it turned out to be not just a passing acquaintance, but an active friendship

75

between them that came to involve a whole lot more than that.

It wasn't until after Lacey Tooker's dog was killed that I began to wonder just what kind of adverse effects that friendship might be having on my Gunar and my Bo. But by then it had already gone way too far, and it was probably too late for me to do anything at all effective about it. Mrs. Boots had so completely established herself in our household that it was out of the question that I should even consider a move to let her go.

I was never really sure whether Phoebe Tooker envied or only resented the fact that I had a housekeeper. Probably it was a little bit of both. She did say once, long ago, at the beginning of things, that she thought I sure was a lucky one, wasn't I, to have married a man like the Doctor, who could afford to pay for such a luxury. But her implication was not that she was unlucky to be married to a man like Jack Tooker, who believed that his wife ought to be able to do the job herself and who didn't make so much money that there was enough left over to hire a maid anyway. It was more like she was saying that I didn't have it in me to manage things on my own, the way that she was doing, and so it was a good thing for me, and the Doctor and the boys, too, that I didn't have to.

Not that Phoebe was managing things all that well herself. The headaches had begun to plague her already by then—big, booming migraines that left her incapacitated for a whole day long sometimes. She made plenty of visits to the Doctor, but he admitted to me that he could find little wrong and less to do about it. So it would sometimes happen that I would find myself in charge of a whole house full of children—as if my own two boys weren't enough trouble for anyone, there would be the Boots kids and Lacey Tooker besides, all crowded together in the kitchen with their toys.

Now it's been my experience that children can be sensitive to the attitudes of adults toward themselves and their playmates, and they're also quick to pick up and imitate the habits, both bad and good, and the points of view, both myopic and farsighted, of the adults who happen to be closest to them. And so, because Phoebe Tooker felt such disdain, even loathing, for poor little Casey and Neva Jolene, Lacey mimicked her mother's prejudice, but was much less subtle in her expressions of it.

It only worked that way for a while, of course. Years later Lacey would do a sly about-face and take great pleasure in defying her mother, who had become more enemy than model by then, and go and get herself tied up more seriously than ever with that Casey Boots.

Neva Jolene may have been ugly, but she was not stupid. She knew all about how Phoebe and Lacey looked at her as if she really were some kind of a monster, and she was tough enough, even as a skinny little kid, not to let herself get cowed by their disgust. Just the opposite, in fact. To Neva Jolene Boots, the Tookers all high and mighty up there on the hill in their big, white house—never mind about the peeling paint—were an affront and a challenge that she was very much prepared to meet and conquer.

Gunar was twelve years old, Lacey and Casey were ten, and Neva Jolene and Bo were only eight when it happened. Lacey had brought to school three small china dolls that her father had bought for her, and Phoebe had clothed in lovely little dresses that she had sewn herself. After show-and-tell was over and the classes were let out for recess in the morning, Lacey left her dolls tucked safely away, she thought, at the back of her desk. But when the children came back inside again, they found the dolls all smashed and their pretty dresses soiled and torn. Someone—and I'm not going to say it wasn't Bo—had seen Neva Jolene hanging around the classroom when the others were outside and said so to Lacey, who came right out and, through her tears, loudly accused the younger girl of ruining her dolls out of pure malice and spite.

No one knew for sure whether it really was Neva Jolene who had done the deed, but we all had our suspicions, and

Lacey was convinced. So was Phoebe, for that matter, but she was more tactful and much less harsh in her condemnation of Neva Jolene. She even told Lacey that maybe she shouldn't be so angry, and to make some room for forgiveness and spare some pity for that poor girl who was, after all, less fortunate than she, and ugly and mean besides. Phoebe was still going to church every Sunday then, and trying her best to put into practice the lessons that the Bible has to teach.

But Lacey would not let up. And neither would Mrs. Boots. And so Neva Jolene took plenty of abuse from both of them before the whole incident could be said to have blown by and been finally forgotten.

Lacey saw to it that Neva Jolene got sent home from school and lost her recesses for two weeks, which must have seemed like an eternity of faraway laughter and empty classrooms to her. And Mrs. Boots spanked her and starved her and wouldn't let her play outside.

Neva Jolene suffered all of this in silence, until her fury was alive and burning.

Next thing, Bo came home and told me that Lacey Tooker's dog had been killed.

Lacey had this dog, a big furry mutt named Blue that Jack Tooker had found straying half wild and hungry around the slaughterhouse and had brought home as a friend and companion for his girl. Phoebe had had her hysterectomy years back, and so there weren't going to be any brothers or sisters for Lacey. Jack didn't want Lacey growing up too lonely, and he thought that the dog might be just the thing.

At first it looked like a bad idea. Lacey was afraid of the animal. She complained that he smelled. She hated the heat of his breath on her arm when he sat panting at her side. Phoebe griped about the fleas and ticks, the hairs on the sofas and the dirty pawprints on the rug, and she made it a rule that the dog would be kept outside. Blue took to lying out on the front porch, looking wistfully in through the screen door, waiting for Lacey to come outside so that he could follow her around. Or he sat on his haunches in the yard, at the end of the drive, waiting for cars to pass so that he could chase them, barking furiously, reckless and wild, down the hill away from the Tooker Place and into town.

Finally what happened was he was smacked by a pickup truck. It had been snowing, and the road was slick. The boy who was driving the truck told Lacey that if she couldn't keep her dog tied up, she at least ought to teach him not to chase cars. He said it was Lacey's own damned fault if her animal was hurt now. Turned out, he ended up killed himself a few years later when he fell off a mountain in Montana where he had gone to work as a ranger.

Anyway, there was Blue, all limp and bloody in the street. And there was Lacey, all cold and crying in the snow. The boy was awkward, bundled up in his parka, as he tried to lift and carry the big animal to his truck to take it to the vet. Blue's body was so limp and heavy that the boy staggered under the weight, lost his grip in the thick fur, and dropped the dog against the side of the road. It rolled down into the ditch, and the boy would have left it there to die, but Lacey, chastened by the accident and stirred to pity by the animal's snarling pain, climbed down after Blue herself.

She waited there half dressed in the cold, with Blue's head cradled in her lap, looking into his helpless suffering eyes and fingering the velvety flaps of his ears, until Jack came back with a blanket and a vet. The dog had a broken pelvis and spent several months with his hind legs held motionless in a plaster cast. After that he gave up chasing cars, but refused ever to leave Lacey's side. He wouldn't stay out anymore, and if Phoebe tried to close the door on him, he scratched at the screen until he clawed it down.

Phoebe used to have to shut the dog up in the garage to keep him from following down the hill after them when she drove Lacey to school in the morning. And he would be waiting for her, watching the road, when she came back home again at night. He followed her everywhere, lay at her feet, put his head in her lap, slept at the end of her bed.

*   *   *

79

One spring afternoon, not too long after the incident at school with the dolls, Bo came home and said to me, "Mom, Blue got killed!"

The Doctor was in his examining room, giving some farmer's wife the glad news that she was pregnant—which was not such a blessing after all, since she had five little ones already, and when she got home and broke the news to her husband that another one was on the way, he would beat her up so badly that she would lose that baby two days later. I was upstairs touching up the ironing—it was Mrs. Boots's day off, and though she was industrious enough in pursuing her other chores, she just never could please the Doctor with her pressing of his white jackets. And Gunar was still not home from school—which had not yet begun to worry me since he often stayed after for a game of baseball on the schoolyard diamond—when Phoebe called.

She was hysterical, crying and babbling so at first I thought that maybe Lacey had been hurt, too.

"Oh God, Annie, please, the dog . . . Lacey . . . I don't know what to do . . ."

I told her to stay calm. Everything would be fine. I'd get the Doctor, and we'd be right there.

Of course when we got to the Tooker Place we saw that it wasn't Lacey who was hurt, it was only Blue. He was dead, lying on the front porch, flies buzzing in his eyes, his tongue lolling on the floorboards, the bowl of food nearby half gone. It looked like he'd been poisoned, the Doctor said, examining Blue's eyes.

"Lacey's locked herself in her room," Phoebe moaned, wringing her hands, looking away, trying not to see the dog's body on her porch. "What do I do now?"

I stood outside Lacey's door and pleaded with her to let me in. She screamed at me to go away. It wasn't until Jack came and talked to her that she agreed to come out. She fell into Jack's arms. The Doctor took a look at her and then gave her some Valium to settle her down.

"You know she said it was Neva Jolene," Phoebe told me as she poured out the coffee downstairs. Outside the men were having the animal carried away. Jack put it into the trunk of his car and he and the Doctor drove it to the vet's to be destroyed. "I don't know how she knows that. She didn't see. She just said she knows, that's all. And I wouldn't be surprised, Annie. I wouldn't put it past that kid."

I tried to tell Phoebe otherwise. I said maybe it was a neighbor or a stranger or somebody else. Maybe it was somebody who wanted to rob the house and had to get rid of the dog first.

Phoebe looked at me and rolled her eyes. She didn't believe that for a minute, and neither did I. Wizen River didn't have robbers. There wasn't much crime around here then.

"Okay, so what if it was Neva Jolene?" I asked. "What can you do about it? You don't have any proof. She's just a little kid. How could you turn her in? What would you say? Who would you tell? And anyway, what good in the world would it do?"

Phoebe shrugged. She could see what I was saying. She knew what I meant. Probably she was just as glad to be rid of the animal anyway.

Jack wasn't satisfied, though. He went to Mrs. Boots and told her what had happened. According to Jack, Neva Jolene denied the whole thing, and Casey backed her up. Mrs. Boots looked at Jack Tooker and then she looked at her children.

"Poison?" she said.

"They put it in his food," Jack answered. He was holding his hat in his hand and shifting from one foot to the other, trying to contain his outrage, trying to hold back his pain.

Mrs. Boots laughed. "Where in the world would these kids get anything like that?"

Casey and Neva Jolene stared at Jack, daring him to answer.

He looked around the shabby room and shook his head.

"I don't know," he said. "But they got it somewhere."

81

He turned to the children and stooped to confront them face to face. "I know you got it somewhere. I know you did it. Don't be fooled. Just because you're kids doesn't mean you're not guilty as devils in my eyes."

Mrs. Boots showed him the door, and he went home to his daughter and his wife.

"It was only a dog," Phoebe told him.

Upstairs, Lacey was asleep.

It wasn't until a few weeks had gone by and everybody had pretty much forgotten about Blue and how he died that the Doctor discovered the half bottle of barbiturates missing from the shelf in his office.

I told him I had taken them. I lied, and I said that it was me. I needed them for my flowers, I said. I read somewhere that sleeping pills brighten their blooms. He believed me. He couldn't imagine any reason that I might have to lie.

I guess I know now I ought to have done something to my boys. I knew that they had helped Casey and Neva Jolene. They had stolen those pills, and even if it was those Boots kids who put the drugs in the dog's food, still my boys were just as responsible for Blue's death. I should have let them know I knew. I should have told Phoebe and Jack and made my boys stand up and take whatever punishment and humiliation might be their due.

But I couldn't do it. I loved them too much. Is that so very different? Is that so terribly wrong? My job was to protect them, even if it did mean I had to lean too close, hover too near. There was nothing else for me to do but keep them from getting hurt any way I could. Even if it meant I had to lie. Even if it meant I would look the other way and pretend I hadn't seen. Keep my hands in my pockets and pretend I didn't know.

Maybe I was hoping that somehow they would punish themselves, just knowing that what they had done was wrong. They had heard Lacey crying. They had seen the way she was afterward, pale and lost and sad in a way that made her face look more beautiful than it ever had.

82

I just could not bear to see Bo or Gunar hurt. Not in any way. Not for any reason. No matter if they deserved their pain or not.

I guess I know now that I hushed it up a little too well. Because Lacey had the time to forgive and to forget. Six years later she went and lost sight of everything she knew. She let herself fall in love with that Casey Boots, and she forgave him for the fact that he had one time helped his sister poison her beloved Blue.

7

The Man Named Casey Boots Who Is Your Father

PATRIS EST FILIUS

Casey Boots and Lacey Tooker were just fifteen years old when they first stole off together into the trees in Center Park, that summer when the tornado ripped in from the fields and took the steeple to the Lutheran church with it as it stormed its way back out again. And all of us who saw them together afterward had to admit that they sure did make a pretty pair, those two. That was because they were so much alike—they looked more like brother and sister than he and Neva Jolene ever would, and in a town any more populated than Wizen River, where everybody didn't already know better, they might have been mistaken for siblings. They both had that thick, black hair—Casey's was short and curly like his truant dad's, and Lacey's was long and straight like her mother's—and bright blue eyes that were still innocent enough for you to be able to see in them whatever it was that might be on their minds.

But to say that they looked good together was not the same thing as giving your approval to their pairing. Phoebe sure never did anything remotely close to that in her lifetime. Even though Casey Boots seemed, to the rest of us at least, to have grown up into a nice enough young man by then, still Phoebe had not, like her fickle daughter, forgotten just what fate Blue had met in what she suspected were at least partly Casey Boots's hands. Her memory was good enough to make her believe that no matter how pleasant and polite and downright handsome he might seem to be, Casey Boots had in him a badness that would sure enough show itself one day and bring down some kind of big trouble onto anybody standing close enough to be caught by it, too.

Phoebe was only looking after her daughter's welfare— no more nor less than any mother might be expected to do—and she didn't want her Lacey to be involved when that one day finally rolled around. And if Jack Tooker didn't join in with his wife's adamant condemnation of the whole affair just then, that was only because he was already having enough troubles of his own, what with changing his job from the slaughterhouse to insurance and trying to keep his hair from going gray at the same time.

Although Phoebe never actually went so far as to forbid her daughter to see that Boots boy at all—that would have been a taboo too completely irresistible and anyway too hard to enforce in a town so small as Wizen River—she did do her best to make sure that Lacey was in his company as little as possible and always supervised when it couldn't be avoided altogether.

Casey Boots was not allowed up to the Tooker Place at all, and yet it's easy enough to see now that everybody would have been better off for it in the end if he had been. Anyway, hindsight is easy. For all her trouble all Phoebe managed to really do was force Lacey to go to pretty elaborate lengths just to keep the flames of her young romance with Casey Boots fanned and burning bright.

It wasn't all that easy for my own boys, either, when Lacey and Casey picked up on each other like that and started to get so serious about it so fast. Gunar and Bo had, over the years, kept up their good friendship with Casey Boots, and when he started to see so much of Lacey Tooker all the time, that broke into their threesome and made things awkward enough for everybody so that my boys ended up out in the cold. It was hardest on Bo, of course, because he was still too young to be getting into any real messes with girls himself yet, and because he liked Casey so much, almost as much as he admired his own brother, and because he had a good, hard schoolboy crush on Lacey Tooker back then with the rest of them, too. It couldn't have made him feel any too good to be standing by, too young and too shy and too awkward, while Lacey was smiling back at that Casey all the time.

There were a few times, in the beginning when it was still summertime and all of this was brand new, that the four of them would go hanging around together. That was fine with Phoebe—she had always hoped that her daughter might someday see her way clear to falling for one of my boys—and so it was a convenient cover-up for Lacey, too. Bo swallowed whatever was left of his adolescent pride, just to keep company with her, and later she started to count on his loyalty so much that he turned into the go-between for her and Casey after it came out that she was pregnant and Phoebe had a more urgent interest in seeing to it that the two of them were kept away from each other for good.

Lacey Tooker never saw the ragged hole that Bo slammed into his bedroom wall with his bare fist, just there behind the door, on the night he heard that she would be leaving, going off to California to have Casey's baby in a home for unwed mothers.

The boys had begun to come sniffing around Neva Jolene by then, too, and because she was still such an ugly little thing, with that horrid blotch staining half her face as if it were some kind of a strawberry fungus that had attached itself and was growing there on her skin, she was counting herself lucky to be having any boyfriends at all, and she wasn't too particular either about who was taking her off into the trees after dark in Center Park. She was, at fourteen years old, crossing bridges that burned up in flames behind her, giving away pieces of herself that she would never again be able to get back. And everybody knew about it, too, except maybe her mother, who always had been deaf and dumb when it came to any bad news about her girl.

Casey couldn't have cared less. It hadn't taken him very long in his life to learn the lesson that it was always best to keep Neva Jolene busy and out of his hair. He offered his sister up freely to his friends and considered they were doing him a favor when they took him up on it and carried her away.

Of course, Casey and Lacey had to meet every day at school—there wasn't any way in the world of getting around that. But then Lacey would go on and drag it deeper and make it all much worse with the fabulous stories that she concocted for her mother to explain where she had been or where she was going and why she could promise that Casey Boots hadn't been or wouldn't be there, too. And it just happened to be about the same time that Jack Tooker started kicking up trouble of his own for Phoebe, and she got so distracted by that and had her hands so full with him that she wasn't able to keep such close track anymore of all Lacey's comings and goings. She hoped that I would do that for her, but I never made any promises and I never said I would. She just assumed that I felt the same as she did. Just like she assumed that Jack would never leave.

Then, before anybody knew what had happened, Lacey Tooker was pregnant and Jack was dead.

Now, nine years later, Phoebe Tooker had gone and driven her Chevy off the road and up a tree and into the ditch, and she was dead, too. And Lacey had come back, with her boy John, from their exile in California, to listen to the eulogy and see her mother put into the ground.

The morning after the funeral, I got a phone call, and it was Lacey Tooker. She wanted to know if maybe it would be all right and not too much trouble to borrow my car for just a while that day to go down into town to do a little sight-seeing—visiting the old places and stomping grounds, reliving the memories, recalling the times. I told her that she could have Bo's car while she was in town. It had been shut up in our garage for a long time. I told her I would be up the hill for her in a little while.

Now that Lacey Tooker was back in Wizen River again, there was not much chance that Bo would be caught moping around, sleeping in, or feeling punk at home. I guess he had been up fretting and scheming half the night before, looking for some kind of a plan that would bring him into a romantic chance encounter with Lacey, and he was truly relieved and, I think, thrilled when I put an end to all of that by telling him that she had just that morning phoned about the car.

He frowned and looked away from me, searching the room, ceiling to floor, I'm not sure for what exactly, and pulled that baseball cap down lower on his head—so that even his eyebrows were hidden beneath its rim—and he chewed on his knuckle for a while. Then he smiled crookedly and said that, well, maybe he should be going on up the hill there with me, you know, so he could explain to her about the car and everything.

And then he really got excited and sat right up straight and slapped both hands down flat on the table and nodded and grinned, spittle gathering white in the corners of his mouth, and he said, "Like the window, you know, how it always sticks a little there on the driver's side, unless you're careful and you roll the thing real slow-like and gentle . . ."

And what did I think? Shouldn't Lacey be prepared for a thing like that? Wasn't it only fair?

Lacey was standing out on the front porch, expecting us, and I thought that she must have been up in her bedroom window watching us as we drove up the hill and then scampered downstairs and out the door when we pulled into the drive. She was looking a whole lot better than she had the day before—not so tired, not so haggard, not so worn out by travel and bad news. Maybe it was just that she was happy, even relieved, to see us.

It could have been the fact of living in that old house again, now that her mother—who had, after all, been her worst enemy—was dead and buried. The ghosts of her parents and her past must have been haunting her, opening up doors that she had for a while anyway been able to keep pretty much closed and locked.

But whatever it was, she was sure smiling now, and she looked beautiful doing it, too. She said hello to me as we approached, and kissed Bo gently on the cheek when we were beside her. She turned gracefully away and led us both back on into the house. She was saying, over her shoulder and through a curtain of hair, that John was still asleep, but she'd been up for hours and hours, it was so strange to be back home.

After all those years.

Inside the house, I noticed that things had already been changed. Even though Phoebe Tooker had never had anyone like Mrs. Boots coming in even once a week to see that the constant battle against confusion and filth was carried on toward at least a temporary victory every day, she had always kept her home tidy and clean enough for strangers, even when Lacey was small and grubby and Jack was still around to add his messes to the rest.

I could see right away that Lacey never would be the careful kind of homemaker that her mother had been. There were clothes lying around, thrown carelessly across the chairs and sofa in the living room. John had hauled out old toys and comic books and left them strewn all over the house. The kitchen sink was stacked up high with dirty dishes. I could imagine Mrs. Boots whirling in there and putting it all right again, but she had retired years ago, a concession to the arthritis that had gnarled up her hands until it was just too painful for her to do much of anything at all anymore.

Bo was grinning so hard and happily at the sight of Lacey Tooker that his cap got pulled all crooked on his head, and I had to reach over and straighten it for him before we sat down together at the kitchen table. Lacey poured coffee, and Bo busied himself with the sugar and cream. The timer on the oven buzzed, startling us enough so that we smiled nervously at each other, and Lacey brought out from the oven a steaming tray of sweet rolls that I recognized as having been baked by Phoebe, probably that very morning a few days ago, just before she set off on her ill-fated drive down the hill to my house and her sudden rendezvous with the oak tree in the ditch.

So, there we were—Lacey, still beautiful, maybe even more so now with nine years to ripen her, sipping her coffee and flipping that fine black hair away from her face; Bo, grinning, all teeth, looking foolish in the old green baseball cap he always wore; and me, feeling uncomfortable and maybe even just the tiniest bit ashamed to be munching on my dead friend's warmed-over bakery with the daughter that she had so despised.

Our chitchat had been meaningless and pleasant and light until Bo started in about the funeral and how surprised he had been to hear what Father Phil had to say about what had really caused the accident, and it was just about then that Lacey went off into her own rant about the dog in the road and the *I Brake for Animals* sticker on the bumper of the Chevy and how that dog had to have been there just then, crossing over from one part of the woods to the other, to drive her mother off the road and into the trees like that. She was just finishing up rolling her eyes at me when the doorbell rang.

It turned out to be John who answered it. He just happened to be the one who got there first, that's all. He must have been on his way downstairs—maybe he'd been drawn up and out of his dreams and his bed by the sweet smell of Phoebe's rolls—when the bell rang, and so, naturally, he turned back and opened the door. We all heard the bell, and we all heard John's shout, and, though it sounded friendly enough to me, Lacey went white with fear. I guess she must have been remembering her intruder in California and for a moment fancied that he had somehow possessed both the will and the means to follow her halfway across the country just to finish up whatever tortures he had had in mind for her that evening when my telegram came and offered Lacey the strongest possible excuse to escape.

But, after all, this was Nebraska now and not California. And Bo and I, at least, were pretty sure that whoever it was at the door was someone who came with friendly intentions. Bo was still grinning, and his cheeks were all puffed out with pastry, making him look even more ridiculous as he chewed and slurped his coffee and grinned at me and looked at Lacey and shook his head, as if it were just about all he could do to contain his glee and keep himself from sputtering out a laugh that would have sent out a fine spray of crumbs and coffee. And then I figured out why Bo was so tickled by everything that had happened so far, and that was because it was none other than Casey Boots himself who came tromping on after John back into the kitchen.

"Well, well," he said. "Good morning, Annie D. And look who's back in town."

John turned and looked up at his father as if to let him out of his sight would be to make him disappear again altogether. The boy was still in his pajamas, big baggy flannel things that hung down over his feet and could have tripped him up and made him fall. Casey put his hand down on John's head, weaving his fingers in through the boy's sleep-snarled hair, just as I had seen his mother do to him so many years before.

Casey had his eye on Lacey. She stood with her back to the sink, her hair thrown away from her face and her chin stuck up and her hands on her hips, ready to meet and defeat any challenge that might decide to come her way—that had, in fact, already in the form of Casey Boots, come up the hill to take a peek at the boy who everybody had been saying was his son.

We were watching Lacey, then, each of us looking for some sign from her that would put us back at ease again. Bo had his coffee cup lifted halfway to his mouth, and he was frozen like that with the thing suspended midway between the table and his lips, which were still pulled back into a goofy grin, though he had at least stopped his giggling and was quiet now.

Lacey stared at Casey. She had her eyes all over him, studying him from the top of his head right down to his shoes, looking and looking, drinking in the sight of him like somebody who's just been dying of thirst.

"John," she said, finally pulling herself away from Casey to look her son slow and steady in the eye, "this man here is Casey Boots. He's your dad."

John held Lacey's look, solemn and understanding, until she turned away to fuss at the sink with some of those dishes that had been left there overnight. He hitched up the pants of his pajamas and faced Casey Boots. "Pleased to meet you, sir," he said, his voice cracking with the awkwardness of it.

Casey threw back his head and laughed out loud. John, confused, looked to his mother for help, but she kept her back to him, her elbows out and head bent, water running hard over her hands. Casey just went on laughing, his eyes filling up with tears that he rubbed away with the back of his hand, his breath hitching and catching, until finally John was smiling, too, just at the sight and the sound of it. Casey had been standing in the doorway all this time, and he took two long steps into the room and across to John. He bent over the boy and picked him up, holding him high and helpless, all flailing arms and legs, then brought him back close again, so close that John moaned against the pressure of Casey's hard embrace.

By that time Casey wasn't laughing anymore. His face was all twisted up into an agony of sorrow and joy, and tears were filling up in his eyes. He set the boy back down, carefully placing him on his feet, and turned away.

"I'm sorry," he mumbled. He took a deep breath. "Too early in the morning for this," he said. "Too hard of a way to start out the day."

Lacey turned off the tap and fixed him a cup of coffee.

She pressed it into his hands and nudged him toward the table.

"Sit down, Casey," she said. Her voice was a melody, a bird song, as Casey took a seat next to Bo. The chair legs scraping the floor were like a scream.

Casey smiled at John. "I guess I just never heard anybody call me 'sir' quite like that before," he said. John bowed his head and looked at his bare feet against the linoleum. "But it sounded pretty good," Casey went on. "Especially coming from a fine boy like you." Casey looked around at all of us. "I mean that," he said. He wrapped his hands around the warm mug and studied its steaming depths.

John, guessing that his father had just paid him some kind of a roundabout compliment, beamed at his mother and helped himself to one of Phoebe's rolls.

Looking at the two of them, Casey and John, I had to say the boy had his father's face.

Though that first meeting between Lacey and Casey and their boy John had its clumsy moments—like when they both started up talking at the same time, just to fill up the gap of silence that kept falling in between their awkward observations about the weather and the house and Phoebe's death and how the town had maybe changed or maybe stayed the same—even so, the heat was there. It was a fire whose coals had been banked, but not extinguished altogether after all that time apart. It didn't seem like anything at all had been lost between those two. Casey was looking at Lacey as if he could just taste the skin that shone beneath her clothes. And Lacey was looking back at him as if she could feel the ripple and play of muscle in his shoulders and his arms.

John's presence flowed between them like cool water.

I guess it was probably made all the more difficult for everybody by the fact of my being there with Bo, sipping coffee and listening in and watching them like some nosy old busybody. Here were Lacey Tooker and Casey Boots, who had not seen but maybe had been thinking of each other over the last nine years, and their son, a family reunited, refugees from a tornado named Phoebe, whose fierce, protective love had torn them apart and kept them that way until she died.

I thought I'd better go, but I would leave Bo behind with them. That was important, and it took him by surprise. He hadn't been out of my sight for a very long time. But it just seemed all right to me. He was so happy to be back in the company of these friends of his again. Like old times. As if nothing much had changed.

"Stick around," Casey said to Bo. "Don't go running off."

"Be careful . . ."

"I'll watch him, Annie D. I'll take care of him. He'll be fine." Casey put his arm around Bo's shoulders and shook him gently.

"Bring him back . . ."

It was agreed that Bo would be brought back down to the house later and that they could pick up his car for Lacey then.

Lacey walked out to the drive with me. The air was warm, with just a promise of the more oppressive summer heat to come, and there in the drive Lacey hesitated, looked at me square, and asked about Bo.

"What is it? Is he all right? He looks so, well, different," she said, groping, trying hard to understand. "He doesn't seem the same."

She was so pretty and so young, so curious and so concerned, and I had to look away.

She hurt my eyes, that girl.

I couldn't bring myself to tell her the truth just then. Not after what I had seen. So I tried to brush it off and away with one quick sweep of my hand. I looked up into the trees overhead—they were just leafing out for summer—and I told her Bo was going to be fine.

"Nothing to worry about," I said. "Nothing, really."

"But . . ." She frowned and tried to get me to tell her more.

"You've been gone a long time, Lacey," I told her. "Things happen; people change," I said.

That was all.

And then I smiled and climbed into my car and drove back out of the drive, away from the Tooker Place and down the hill, past the skinned oak that had been the death of Phoebe and was so damaged it would probably be dead itself soon, too, into town and back to my own house by the river. I left Lacey with her hands in her pockets, standing there in the drive. I let her keep all her questions to herself. I gave them all right back by answering nothing at all.

Of course, I knew it wouldn't last. I did know and could admit that much at least. I knew that Lacey Tooker would be getting all her answers soon enough; that she would be hearing the whole story from Casey Boots; that he would be the one to tell her about how my son, Bo, wasn't well, that he had gone a good long way toward killing himself, and if he was different now because of that, well, he was lucky anyway that he was still alive at all.

8

The Truth About Phoebe Tooker

MATER DOLOROSA

The baby that had Phoebe Tooker all swelled up out of shape for those few months back when Jack came home from the war—before I met and married the Doctor—was lost into the toilet one early morning after they had moved up the hill into the house that would come to be called the Tooker Place when they had lived in it long enough, wasn't really a baby at all.

It was a lump.

Phoebe had all the signs, but the Doctor told me later that he had it in her records that the thing had been some kind of a mole. He used a long and complicated word that was built up out of too many odd syllables for anybody but a doctor to remember, but it started out something like a hydra, and I do recall that part because of the monster that the word brought to my mind the first time that I heard the Doctor name it. And my imagination wasn't too far off the mark, either.

Even little Casey Boots, for all his terror, had not been able to dream up a thing so hideous and malformed as what was brought forth from Phoebe Tooker's womb four years ahead of Lacey. That mole was not, according to the Doctor, who told me all about it over our luncheon one of those days after we were married and before Gunar was born, just an ordinary clump of errant cells.

It had hair.

And teeth.

Phoebe carried that thing there inside of her for four whole months before she found out that it wasn't a baby. I, for one, thought that she sure did seem to be getting pretty big pretty fast, and I said so, too, but old Eli Johnson, the doctor—who was thoughtful enough to pass over the next spring, leaving behind him the place in Wizen River that Dr. Diettermann would come to fill—kept insisting that she looked just fine to him. He'd seen plenty of pregnant ladies in all his years of practice, and every one of them was a different story to tell. No two the same. Or maybe it was twins, he admitted finally, when even he had to agree that Phoebe sure was big for being only a little more than a third of the way gone. And poor Jack Tooker—I do think that he happily envisioned a whole litter of babies in there, and he was all set to have them come fill up his house.

"The more the merrier," he said.

It really wasn't until Phoebe started to bloat right out with all that water, as if she were some kind of a grotesque blow-up balloon, so that her fingers filled up and her rings cut right into them, and she couldn't even wedge her feet into her shoes anymore at all, that Eli Johnson and Jack Tooker started thinking that something might not be right about it after all. And then when she was bleeding, finally, and passed that awful thing into the toilet—Jack had to fish it out and wrap it up in some tissue and a towel—they took her off to the hospital in Omaha to have whatever was left over up there scraped away then with the rest. Like cleaning out the meat of an acorn squash, I think.

Everybody else in Wizen River thought that Phoebe Tooker had just had an ordinary miscarriage. It was only Eli Johnson and the Doctor and Jack Tooker and Phoebe herself and I who ever knew the truth about what happened.

And then, of course, after it was all over and Phoebe had got back to normal again, she was desperate to get herself really pregnant this time. She did want to be able to give Jack the babies that he was wishing for, and everybody had heard Jack Tooker tell about how he was planning to raise up a whole gaggle of kids. That was, he said, the very reason that he had gone and got all high and mighty with Phoebe's money by buying that big old white house up there on the hill in the first place. He meant to fill it up with kids.

That wasn't the way that it was going to go for him, though.

Maybe it was just that they were both so anxious about it all. Anyway, it wasn't until four years later, after Eli Johnson was gone and had been replaced by Dr. Dietter-mann, and I had changed from Annie Plant to Annie D., and my own son Gunar was a toddler, that Phoebe Tooker came in for her examination and went home again with the good news that she was pregnant, finally.

Oh, and then how she fussed and fretted about whether it was the real thing this time, up until the day that Lacey kicked her good and hard between the ribs and made it clear to anyone who might have had any doubts about it that it was not some hydra-headed mole this time that was puffing Phoebe up, but Lacey, who would grow up into bigger trouble for her mother than any kind of tumor ever had been or would be either, until worse came to worst and she was pregnant herself and had to be sent away and then didn't even come back again until poor Phoebe was dead—just in time to see her mother buried.

It was while I was on my way down the hill from the Tooker Place up there in the woods—the same morning that Casey Boots showed up and he and his boy John got their first taste of one another and Lacey finally screwed up the nerve to ask outright about Bo, but got nothing from me—driving past the dying old oak and all of that, to my own house down low by the river, following just the same route that my old friend Phoebe had taken, or anyway begun to take, only a few days before, that all those memories about me and Phoebe came washing back into my mind just as though they were the Wizen River itself, trickling along cool and quiet until some storm came along and rained down into it so long and so hard that the water comes rushing in and flooding up over its banks and into the woods behind my house.

I went on my way down home, and I sat out back in the garden—which was steaming in the hot sun and smelled thick with the soil and the manure, because I had just tilled and planted and the seedlings were even beginning to poke up into sight—and I enjoyed the unexpected freedom that Casey Boots had given me when he agreed to look after Bo for the day. I was thinking about Phoebe Tooker, who had, for a lot of different reasons, missed out on some things by being who she was and dying when she did, not the least of which was the sight of her grandson John and his father Casey when they embraced so dear that first time up there in the kitchen with the coffee and the sweet rolls and Bo laughing and Lacey suspicious and me gaping and looking on.

Phoebe had not had much in the way of a family herself. She didn't have any brothers or sisters at all. Maybe that was it. But I had been an only child, too. Still, I had had a mother, for whatever Mona Plant may have been worth to me then, though surely there were times when I wished that I, too, could have been somehow left a half-orphan and spared most of what went along with having Mona around as my mother. Evie Wink had gone into the hospital when Phoebe was five. And she never did come back out.

No one was able to really say for sure what it was that finally went wrong with Evie Wink. She was crazy, that much everybody knew. Maybe it was a disease, inherited, or brought on by some kind of vitamin deficiency. Or maybe it was just that she got tired. Maybe she just let go, stopped trying to be so perfect all the time, in every way. She wore the best clothes, she had the best house, her linens were starched and white, her clothes were beautiful, her hair was lovely and full. Her feet were dainty and small, her hands were soft, her eyes were clear, her skin was smooth. All the other women envied her. She gave off such an aura of comfort and well-being. She made you wish that your life was as well ordered, as wonderful, as perfect as hers seemed to be. It must have made her tired—keeping up appearances, living up to expectations.

There were some people who thought when she went crazy that she deserved it. Anyway, that was what they said.

Phoebe Tooker would foreshadow her own daughter's dog-in-the-road theory by making up a story of her own and then pressing it on everybody for so long that finally only the most stubborn of us still put up a fight when someone started to tell about how Mr. Wink, the banker, had caught poor Evie, who must not have been as happy or as perfect as everybody thought, in a compromising position with that young teller the weekend before she dropped out of the real world altogether by entering a catatonic state that went on for three days and left her sitting in the dark in a corner with her knees pulled up tight against her chest.

What Phoebe loved about her version of the story was that it was romantic, even though she would be blind to the romance of her own daughter's story many years later.

Anyway, what it all came down to meaning for young Phoebe Wink was that Evie was sent away to an institution in Omaha and Phoebe was left without a mother to bring her up right. She had to stay on there with a father, who, though he was always sure to have plenty of cash—which he paid out handsomely to the women who came into Wizen River off the farms to look after Phoebe until she was old enough to look after herself—never seemed to be able to afford the time that it took to bring up a devoted daughter.

Phoebe must have known things. She must have seen. Mr. Wink was a handsome man, and rich. There are women in the world who will give everything they have to a man like that. And then some.

So, it wasn't a surprise to any of us when Phoebe dropped

out of high school just so she could go off and marry that Jack Tooker. She knew a thing or two about love. She had a rare understanding of men.

Jack Tooker was good-looking all right. I guess that just about every girl in Wizen River and miles around had taken a look at him and then thought about maybe gazing up dreamy into those deep green eyes of his and saying yes. He was a real farm boy, too. His daddy had a little land out there to the east of town, not too far south of my father Harley's place.

Now those farm boys, most of them anyway, used to get themselves all dressed up whenever they had to make a trip into town, even when it was just for something simple like school. They still do that, too. It's as if none of them ever wants to be taken for what he really is, which is a farmer. And that's only because everybody else but the farmers, who know better, is always talking about how any man who has to get his living out of the dirt must be just too stubborn or stupid to be doing anything more civilized, like selling cars or life insurance. Some of those farm boys tried so hard to cover up the smell of manure that followed them around everywhere like a cloud of bad luck that they sometimes ended up more dandified in their daddies' after-shave than even the most urbane of the town boys. Harley Plant was never like that, though, and neither was Jack Tooker. He wore his overalls right into school, and his muddy boots, too. He never tried to hide anything. Didn't need to. And everybody loved him all the more for it besides.

Anyway, Jack and Phoebe were sweethearts when she was in high school, and even though Mr. Wink maybe disapproved, he didn't do too much to make things turn out any differently than they did. Maybe he thought that Phoebe deserved a man as simple as Jack Tooker was. Or maybe he had other things on his mind. At any rate, for whatever reason, Mr. Wink didn't lift one finger to stop his only daughter Phoebe from marrying Jack Tooker even before she had graduated from high school.

Women didn't need education then. They only needed strength.

But it doesn't matter anyway. Mr. Wink wouldn't have been able to stop them even if he had taken the time to try. Phoebe could be just as big a mule as her own daughter turned out to be, and she sure had her heart set on Jack Tooker. And she sure did get her way.

No one was too surprised about his side of the story, either. Phoebe Wink was a good catch for any man. First off, she was rich, by Wizen River standards anyway, and she was pretty, too. She was short and plump, but that was more fashionable then than it is now, when all the girls are doing their best to look like cornstalks—and she wasn't fat anyway, more like wholesome-looking, with skin you wouldn't mind touching, just to feel how soft. And then, too, she had all that hair, long and black. She never cut it at all, and she kept it a mystery by pinning it up in the back with a mouthful of copper pins. And those blue eyes, pulled up wide open so she all the time looked like the world had sneaked up from behind and taken her by surprise.

Never mind that her mother was insane.

Turned out, Phoebe Tooker didn't age all that well. Her hair lost its gleam over the years, and her rosy round face paled and fell, sagged right down with the forces of gravity and time and tugged the corners of her mouth along with it so that between those arched eyebrows and her continual frown, she looked always startled and annoyed, both at the same time, like someone whose child had crept up and touched the back of her neck, just there in the fold below where the wisps of new hair come in, with a wet, cold, and sticky kiss.

That would be Lacey. Phoebe ended up blaming just about everything that happened on her. Whatever went wrong, it was Lacey's fault. Even when Jack finally felt he'd had enough and walked. That, according to Phoebe, was because he and Lacey just got so close—like that, she said, holding up two fingers pressed tight together, intertwined—and there wasn't ever enough of him left over for her. And, if that wasn't enough, it had to be all those wild kids of Lacey's own generation who went and stole the whole show away with their ideas about love and peace and all of that, and in the process led good, stable workingmen like Jack Tooker far astray and off the beaten path.

The troubles between Phoebe and Lacey went way back to when Lacey was an infant. Because Phoebe had been an only child, she had no idea at all about what it would mean to have a baby around the house. When the rest of the town girls were earning their own spending money with baby-sitting jobs, Phoebe was running around with Jack Tooker. She was the first one to have a real boyfriend, and he was three years older, besides. But then she found out, when Lacey was born, that she hadn't been at all prepared for the consequences of her love. The demands that maternity made on her and the endless sacrifice and responsibility of motherhood were nearly unbearable for the likes of Phoebe Tooker.

To make matters worse even than that, Lacey was not what anyone would call a cooperative child. She had the colic at first and cried all the time. Dr. Diettermann treated that with a dose of bourbon for both the mother and the child and explained that it was due at least in part to Phoebe's own nervousness and excitability. And then when Lacey got over that, she just wouldn't give her mother any kind of a break by napping in the afternoons and going to bed at a decent hour at night. At two years old, Lacey was indomitable and rambunctious. She talked early and then more than anyone wanted to hear. By the time she was three, she could count all the way up to one thousand and back down again, and she would do it, too, if you let her, with her knees locked and her feet planted firm, her hands clasped behind her back and her chin slightly tilted, her eyes filmed over so that she looked like she might be blind.

It was as if Phoebe and Lacey, though mother and daughter, were made of such different stuff that they could never be reconciled, and just the slightest little thing that one did could set the other right on edge. Phoebe had been grateful when the Doctor agreed to recommend the hysterectomy. By that time she was happy to go to any lengths at all to make sure that she would never have to bear and raise another child. Any lengths short of celibacy, that is. She wouldn't have been able to say no to Jack.

So what she had done was to come in and see the Doctor again and again, complaining about how her hips just ached and ached.

"Vell, vere exactly does it hurt?" the Doctor would ask her. "And vat is da pain like?"

"Here," Phoebe would answer, pressing her fingers against the soft pouch of her lower belly. "And here. It's like something's gnawing me. Eating. It hurts like teeth. Gnawing."

"Maybe I don't know, Annie, but to me it seems like all da pain comes right from here," the Doctor said to me, pointing to his head, "and here." He put his hand, fingers spread, flat against his chest, above his heart.

And what went on after the surgery was over was even worse. Phoebe seemed to have enjoyed the luxury of her stay in the hospital, being waited on hand and foot by all those competent, efficient, businesslike, and sympathetic nurses and no kid around to eat away at her soul with demands on her attention. By the time she came home to Wizen River again, Phoebe's pelvic pains had spread, compounded by headaches and fevers and fainting spells besides. She worried constantly about getting fat or growing a beard or going insane or turning frigid because of her operation.

It was almost as if Phoebe had come to be in need of her pain. It turned into a way of life for her, and without it I think she would truly have been lost. There wouldn't have been much point to her life anymore. That was what Lacey had meant when she told me she thought that maybe Phoebe was, after all, glad about Lacey's getting pregnant and all, because it was more trouble, and it just seemed like trouble was what kept Phoebe wound up and ticking. Maybe her life had got to be too easy, too simple, too painless, with Jack dead and Lacey gone, and that and not any stray dog was the real reason the Chevy ended up where it did. Maybe it was something like Evie Wink being so tired that the darkness in the corner of the room seemed as good a way out as any.

Anyway, what Phoebe came away from Omaha with was what she described many times as a dull, gnawing, achy feeling just there—and she would indicate her lower belly and her hips with a vague sweep of her hand—and the terrible headaches that overcame her whenever there was any kind of crisis, and often even when there wasn't. It was, she said, as if her whole body was mourning the loss of an important organ. I think the truth was that she just needed all that attention. And Jack was happy enough to give it to her. At first, anyway. Probably he figured it was somehow all his fault.

For loving her too much. For wanting her too much. For needing her more than she could stand.

It was Jack who tried to take over with Lacey where Phoebe had left off. When he was still working there at the slaughterhouse, sometimes he'd bring her by just to show her off to all his friends. He did his best to teach her the things he thought it was important for her to know—the difference between right and wrong, the meaning of friendship, the purpose of love. He wanted her to be caring and generous and kind, even if it meant he had to discipline her a little bit now and then. And it was his arguments with Phoebe on this point that seemed to put the first real chinks into the already weakening foundation of their marriage.

"A girl should know enough to stay out of trouble in school," Jack would complain if a note came home about Lacey's conduct in the classroom. She had a tendency to talk too much—she was friendly and she was smart, and she always seemed to have something to say, even though the teachers didn't always appreciate her comments.

"They're just jealous of her, Jack," Phoebe said. "They're jealous of me and always have been, so they take it out on her."

When it looked like Lacey was going to lose the fifth grade spelling bee over the word "cantaloupe," Phoebe went out and found a dictionary with an alternate spelling— "canteloupe"—just as Lacey had said. If one of the girls complained that Lacey had called her a name and made fun of her shoes, Phoebe was right there to argue that the girl must be mistaken, her shoes *were* ugly, too.

"You can't always be protecting her," Jack said to Phoebe.

"If I don't do it, Jack, who will?" Phoebe would be there for her daughter the way her own mother had not.

And then some.

Of course, nobody knew much about any disagreements between the two of them back then. A person would have had to bring herself in pretty close to see the flaws. The Tookers looked to all of us like just about the most successfully matched pair ever to be conjured up within the limited boundaries of Wizen River, Nebraska. Some people even held them up to each other as an example that could teach us all a lesson about love and family ties. And if Phoebe seemed to be having some troubles with her daughter sometimes, well, that was to be expected, wasn't it? We all had our one- and two-year-olds, and we all knew how they could spoil your day for you sometimes. That came with the territory, is all.

But Phoebe was a fastidious housekeeper and Lacey was always a showpiece in her pretty clothes; Jack and Phoebe looked good together, and smiled lovingly at each other, holding hands and sitting shoulder to shoulder with their heads bowed during prayer time in church. Appearances were kept, and we all could at least appreciate that.

As Lacey grew up, her mother started to be a source of embarrassment and shame to her. Everybody knew all about Phoebe's ailments; she never tried to keep those a secret from anyone. This was part of her image—how she could

106

be in so much pain and so beautiful and strong at the same time. And, although Phoebe cared about Lacey, in principle anyway, she sure didn't keep any love left over for anybody else's kids. She didn't like children in general, is what. And she could find something wrong with everybody—their looks, their manners, their clothes, the way they talked or walked or chewed their food. So Lacey was always having to make up excuses to her friends about why they were never invited up to the Tooker Place to play. Really it was only because Phoebe thought that they were just too noisy and too unruly, even if they were only playing dolls behind the closed door of Lacey's bedroom.

At Lacey's eighth birthday party, when the rules were stretched at her father's insistence—he rented a pony for the kids to ride in circles around the front yard and handed out cowboy hats and ice cream sundaes and bags of M&M's—Phoebe managed to ruin everything. One of the boys—maybe Bo, more likely Gunar—got too rowdy and threw some popcorn at someone and that started everybody to laughing and shouting until Phoebe lost her temper and got so mad that she threatened to send every last one of them home right then and there. Pony rides or no.

"But they're just children," Jack pleaded with her, the cowboy hat lopsided on his head, the ice cream scoop dripping thick and sloppy into the cupped palm of his other hand.

Phoebe turned her back and went upstairs. She phoned Dr. Diettermann and took to her bed with another headache while the pony stood in the shade of the tree out front, nibbling at the pansies Phoebe and Lacey together had planted in the yard.

Jack made up for Phoebe when he could. He tried to teach Lacey some sense of responsibility. But then Lacey got too old for trips to the slaughterhouse anymore and snuggles in her daddy's lap, so Jack let go and tried to find a way to get out, too. As Phoebe became more and more of a malcontent, Jack started looking for an escape from her constant whines and gripes in what could have been the numbing balm of booze. It worked for plenty of other men that way, but not for Jack Tooker. He was not a jolly drunk, but a vicious one, and after he had warmed himself up with a few good belts, he started in on Phoebe. She was weak, she was worthless, she was stupid, she was crazy, she was ugly, and she was mean.

"You're ruining Lacey, Phoebe. It's got to stop. You're ruining us. You've already ruined yourself."

On and on it would go until Phoebe, feisty at first, contemptuous and scornful—"I don't do any of this for myself, you know. I am not a piece of fruit! I live my life for you. And for her . . ."—was worn down, cowed and despondent beneath the tremendous weight of her husband's unwavering abuse. "It was you . . . I only wanted . . . I always tried . . ." Then she would take to her room again, tie a black sleeping mask over her eyes, pull the curtains shut against the sunlight outside, and set the vaporizer to work puffing out clouds of healing, hot steam on the floor beside the bed.

So there was Lacey, shut off up in her room to avoid her mother's constant quibbling; Phoebe, malingering in her bed, swallowing one after another of the placebos and tranquilizers that the Doctor had had made just for her; and Jack, holed up in his office, taking refuge in his work and his drink.

I suppose it was during this hard time for her that Phoebe Tooker and I became bound by our friendship in such a way that was complicated and important to us both.

Phoebe had always been prettier and perkier and better liked all around than I ever hoped to be. I envied her for that. She had it in her, like any kid, to be ruthless and cruel in the ways she'd find to make fun of me. I was just such a plain, odd girl, with my bird legs and Latin declensions, and Phoebe was rounder and a better dancer, too. The truth is that we never really got on until we had to when we were working together down at the Wizen River train station. And then I stepped up out of the mud and married the

Doctor, and that made everything different, too. Phoebe began to think twice about how she judged me. She began to reconsider what kind of an association with each other we might be able to have.

What had started as a mockery—the way she was always saying *Annie Diet-ter-mann* like that, with a slight stretching out and lingering over the last name as if she wanted to say to everybody that if they believed that one, they could believe anything at all—became, because it was so easily accepted by the rest of Wizen River, a begrudging acknowledgment of my new status as the Doctor's wife. And then it got to be that if Phoebe expected to be taken seriously by anybody else, then she had better not be making fun of the likes of me. She went ahead and gave the favor of her true friendship, such as it was, and she trusted me to take it as seriously as she.

I found some satisfaction in her suffering. I was happy to fulfill her need.

When Jack left her and Lacey went away, Phoebe was able to depend on me as a person who would always be receptive to her melodrama, first about her husband drinking and dyeing his hair and changing his job and walking out on her, and then about her daughter's willful refusal to toe the line with that baby. I guess it was just that she saw me to be somebody who could be counted on to listen and, it seemed, moved to offer sympathy and love.

And she was always coming in to see the Doctor, too. It wasn't that Phoebe was ever really ill, exactly. Except for that tumor with the hair and the teeth and the hysterectomy after that, she was in a good state of health overall. That's what the Doctor said, and he would be the one to know. But Phoebe was a neurotic and a hypochondriac to boot, and so she came calling on Dr. Diettermann with one complaint or another, most of which proved, upon inspection, to be strictly, as Darla Williams liked to say, in "that big, empty room upstairs."

Dr. Diettermann was a kind man, and generous, and he

humored Phoebe. He seemed to see, as I did, too, that her need was deep-felt and strong.

What happened, then, was this. Lacey Tooker grew up in spite of her mother and went off into the trees with Casey Boots, and when she came back out again, she was in love with the boy. And there was nothing wrong with that, particularly, until Phoebe poked in and tried to stop it all.

She should have known better. She should have remembered about herself and Jack and how it would have been if Mr. Wink had cared enough to come between them. Or maybe she did remember and maybe that was why. However that part of it may have been, Lacey's part was that she was not about to let her mother ruin things this time around. So she lied, and she told Phoebe that it was Bo.

It was none of my business.

When Phoebe asked, I didn't give her anything true one way or the other. Maybe I knew about Casey Boots, but I never said so to her. I guess she took that to mean that it really was Bo that Lacey was always preening for. I don't know. It wasn't my business.

Anyway, then Lacey got to looking as though she might be pregnant, and we all noticed that, and some even started to say so, and Phoebe just kept hoping that maybe like mother like daughter and this one was a mole, too. But, of course, it wasn't.

It was in my garden that the truth came out into the open, finally. Phoebe and I were sitting there on the bench, and she was fiddling with her watch and sighing and looking up at the clouds and fingering the pins in her hair and sighing again, and then at last she took a breath and told me about how Lacey had been throwing up all the time and was getting so she couldn't even zip up her dungarees anymore, and I had to admit that it sure sounded like a baby to me all right. Phoebe nodded and patted the pins again and then she gave it up and put her hands there in her lap and looked at me straight on and said, "Well, then, it's probably Bo."

What could I say? I knew very well that it wasn't Bo. But, well, I really didn't want to have to be the one to say so to Phoebe. So I just smiled back at her and then I started to do all the fiddling and sighing and looking around myself, because I just knew that she was waiting for me to pipe up and say more. And I was on the very edge of giving in and telling all, admitting everything I knew, when Lacey and Bo came banging out the back door and into the garden themselves.

That was when Phoebe just lit into Bo. I guess she thought that it was what was expected of her, even though we could all see that really she was pleased as punch about the whole situation of her Lacey snagging up my Bo with marriage plans like that.

Lacey just laughed.

"Bo?!" she said, squinting at her mother and showing her teeth. "Bo?!"

And then she covered her mouth and threw back her head and laughed harder, which might have been just a little bit more than the situation called for, because Bo did go and get all gloomy over it later, when he had time to play it back in his mind, to consider, and think.

He would have liked very much for it to have been him. I know that now. It was just as well then that it wasn't.

Lacey stopped sputtering finally and looked at her hands and told Phoebe right out about how it was Casey Boots and it had been him all along.

Phoebe opened her mouth and closed her eyes—and fainted. She just threw up her hands, slumped over, and slid, gentle as a rag doll, off the bench and into the dirt at my feet.

I took Phoebe aside later and told her about how I had heard Darla tell about this clinic out in California where Lacey could have the baby and then give it up and come back home to Wizen River as if nothing had happened at all. Phoebe was interested in knowing all about abortions, too, but it was too late by then for anything like that. She would

111

have had the whole apparatus removed if she could have, just the same way she'd taken care of those things for herself.

Lacey left Wizen River for Los Angeles and had her baby there and started her own little family of two from scratch by severing all ties with us back in Nebraska.

And that's all of it. Phoebe Tooker was, in truth, a snob and a crosspatch, who only used me as a friend when she needed a shoulder she could cry on, or lean on, or faint against.

I turned myself into a vessel for all her bitterness and bile. The truth of it was that I loved to see her suffer. I reveled in her misery. I wallowed in her pain.

And in the end, I was just as happy to be done with all of it finally. It was with some amount of relief that I came to see my old friend Phoebe released from all her pain in the vale of tears that she had made of her life. I wouldn't miss her—dead and buried in the ground.

I left my garden, darkening and cool in the shadows of the late afternoon, and went inside my house to wait for Casey to bring Bo back home.

9

Gunar Goes Off to War; Bo Doesn't

BELLA MATRIBUS DETESTATA

My daddy had a scar on his breast, right there on that soft flat, just below where his shoulder took over and bulged out, veined and rugged, and it was long enough and wide enough that it didn't quite fit under my palm when I slipped my hand in beneath the gray-white knit cotton of his undershirt and pressed it up hard against him. It had been from a burn, he told me. A scalding burn.

The story went that when Harley was still little enough to be getting into that kind of mischief—he was often overlooked, the youngest of the brood, a late-life surprise to both his parents, separated from the nearest of his siblings by a breathless span of fourteen years—his mother had left the arm of a saucepan in which she had been boiling eggs pointed outward from and too close to the edge of the stovetop. Harley had reached up to touch the long, black handle, which I guess to his point of view seemed like a strange and irresistible invitation, closed his fingers over its rounded edge, and tugged at it with all his might until finally it tipped and fell, dumping hot water and coddled eggs all down on top of him. Some of the water soaked

113

through the three layers of shirts that his mother had lapped onto him to keep out the Chicago cold, and it left behind on his fair baby flesh a splash of scar tissue.

No hair would grow there. Harley's scar had a surface texture of something soft and lumpy when you skimmed your finger over it, end to end. And it was always so much more pale than the rest of him, whiter even than those places, like his belly and the soft skin under his arms, that never saw the sun, hidden as they were when he was out there on his tractor, under the protective cover of his overalls and his T-shirts.

All the nerves were dead, he said. He told me that when I touched him there, oh, so soft like that, he never did even know it was happening at all.

That would have been one of those nights in early August or late July, when it got too thick and hot outside or in to be doing much more than just sitting back and stirring up some little breeze with the wide swing that Harley had strung up out there on the front porch.

Mona tried to give it more dignity than it deserved by calling the porch a veranda, even when it really began to sag away from the house so that there was a distinct and growing gap there between it and the doorstep, and what should have been three steps down to the front walk was only two. The whole thing had, along with the rest of that rambling old house, been tacked on to the original two rooms by Weary Shires himself, back in 1888, when he began in earnest to search for a suitably young and fertile and wealthy bride.

We would be sitting all together out there on the porch in the dark, me and Harley side by side on the swing and Mona across from us, six feet away in her white wicker chair, picking up on the breezes that we stirred up with our back-and-forth, and I would lean my head against my daddy's arm and stare out past Mona into the shadowy fields across the road and creep my fingers up under his shirt to where that scar was, fingering it so soft he didn't feel a thing. And Harley would be swinging us back and forth and back and forth, slow and even, and kind of humming to himself at the same time, deep down inside his chest, or murmuring with Mona about one small thing or another until finally I would let myself go and fall asleep. And then Harley would carry me upstairs to my bed and tuck me in tight so that I wouldn't roll out in the middle of the night and crack my head on the hardwood floor.

And the funny thing about all of that turned out to be the fact that my own Gunar had a birthmark, and it was right there in that same soft spot, and it even had that same strange shape and surface, but it was smaller, and I could cover the whole thing up with only my thumb.

It wasn't just the birthmark and the scar all by themselves, though. All around in the way that he grew up to look, after he had all his hair and his teeth and was walking around and sharing with us his own small vision of the world, Gunar Diettermann so closely resembled his grampa Harley Plant that sometimes it just plain gave me a spook. I would be looking at my older boy and seeing my father's own image imprinted there on that face and that body—the same unruly tufted blond hair, the same rough features, and even the same dead white mark there on his breast.

I would climb the ladder up into the attic when the Doctor was too busy and the boys were asleep or out to play, and I would pull out some of those old photos and look at them and into them and see the hint of Gunar standing there next to Mona and me, where it used to only be Harley. Maybe that was why what Gunar could do always came as such a shock. Because he looked so much like his grampa, I kept expecting Gunar to act like Harley, too.

But it was Bo, not Gunar, who had inherited that gentle nature. Bo, who was dark-haired and round-joweled like the Doctor, with none of the Shireses' lank or the Plants' brawn, was the peaceful and gentle one of my two boys. Where Gunar was all rough-and-tumble and noise and dirt, Bo was cautious and calm and quiet and clean. Like his father.

He adored his big brother, too. There was not much in the

115

world that Bo would not do for Gunar. Even when he knew that what he was being asked to do was wrong.

Gunar took advantage of his brother's devotion, too, if the truth be told. That was easy. It was almost as if Bo was in his own way always asking for it, as though he just needed to go and show Gunar still one more time how far he would be willing to go to carry it out for him, and so Gunar was only doing what Bo wanted, is how he saw it. Then it was Bo do this, and Bo do that, and Bo do me just one little favor now, will you? And Bo would scramble around doing all the things Gunar was asking him to do and be happy about it, too, so that it was very hard for me to be angry with Gunar when he went and pushed his little brother just one step too far and landed them both in Dutch with the Doctor.

Like that one time in the examining room with little Neva Jolene Boots, who, though she was still just as ugly as she had ever been, was really not all that little anymore and was sure big enough to know what was what with those two boys and how to put a quick enough stop to it, too. But she didn't do that. And then, after it was all over and they had been caught, she went and put all the blame for everything on poor Gunar, as if he'd been the one parading around in Center Park that summer in those shorts that were tight enough to slice a nice crease up there between her legs— and everybody noticed that, even me.

Bo was only the lookout. And the Doctor knew all too well what had gone on between Neva Jolene and Gunar up there on that table, though he did let the girl go, and he did punish both our boys very well. After he had finished with all the Deutsch ranting and roaring up and down the stairs and in and out of all the rooms—as if he expected to find more obscenities hidden away like that in other parts of the house—so long and so loud that his round face got all red and started looking as if it might just pop this time, he locked them upstairs alone in their own separate rooms, with no food and no drink and not even the toilet, until the lesson had sunk in deep enough to stick. Bo wet his bed;

Gunar peed in a long arc out the window onto the lawn below, killing one of the salmon geraniums that grew there along the walk.

"Those two boys of yours sure do look different from each other, now don't they?" Phoebe Tooker would say, nudging me and squinting off across the grass to where the three children were playing together on the little merry-go-round in the playground at Center Park, Lacey and Gunar riding and shouting, "Faster! Faster!" while Bo pushed, running around and around in the sand. Phoebe would shake her head and cluck and say, "That's right, Annie D., just like night and day, those two." And we would both squint to see them better—Gunar tall and thin, tanned and athletic, with that blond hair too shaggy, and Bo shorter and fatter and darker.

Bo always seemed like he was trying hard to be just like Gunar, too. Sometimes he could be a pest.

"Don't touch me," Gunar would say. "Stop looking at me," he would scowl at Bo across the supper table. "Don't copy me." Until they finally came to blows one night with me screeching for them to quit and the Doctor just egging them on, I thought.

When it was all over, and Bo had a bloody nose that stained the linen tablecloth so that I had to cut it up for rags for Mrs. Boots to use on the windows, and Gunar had a bump there on his forehead, and all those broken dishes and that food spilled and spattered there on the linoleum, the Doctor warned me. He said, "Just you stay out of it dis time, Annie."

Boys will be boys and all of that, and then he chuckled to himself and shook his head, remembering the way those kids had torn into each other so quick like that, muttering over and over what Gunar had said to start it all off in the first place.

"Stop looking at me; don't touch me."

That was all.

*   *   *

117

Nobody was too surprised when Gunar Diettermann went off to Omaha and enlisted with the Marines. That was in 1968, when Jack Tooker had started to drink and worry about his age, the Doctor had already died of cancer, peace talks had opened up in Paris, and we had something like five hundred thousand American boys defending the cause of freedom over in Vietnam.

Gunar graduated from high school, piled into the back of a pickup truck full of boys, drove off to Omaha, and signed himself up with the rest of them.

He was only doing what he thought to be the right thing. He wanted to be a soldier, the kind of man who would be there to fight for his country and everything that was beautiful and free in it. It wasn't that he cared about killing anybody. It was that he had a head full of ideas about honor and duty. He thought that it was very clear what he had to do. He thought that he knew what it meant to fight in a war. He never considered any other alternative; he never went looking for any kind of an escape.

The Doctor was already dead, but it never did occur to Gunar that maybe he could claim me and Bo as his dependents. Or that he could get some kind of a scholarship and go on to college with a student deferment. He wasn't a scholar. And since it seemed inevitable, to him anyway, that he would have to join in the fight somehow and become a part of it just so that the rest of us could sleep sweet at night, he decided to sign up for the very best. And the Marines were lucky to have him.

Gunar Diettermann was still young enough to be immortal then.

I never did understand much of it. My boys tried their best to tell me—Bo would roll his eyes and pull on his nose and take a deep breath and start all over again about the North and the South, the ARVN and the Cong and the Communists and the dominoes—but it never did make enough sense to me that it could ever be a part of the way I myself think about the world and the way things are in it and the way

118

things ought to be. Maybe you just have to be a man to see a thing like that with any real clarity.

I had sure heard enough about it all, though. I had heard about what the First World War had done to my father's point of view and what the Second World War had done to the man that I had married and how all those bad memories and dreams and thoughts had kept him up at night when he should have been curled up next to me, warm, peaceful, and asleep. And what for? Not much was any different now from what it had been before—not that I could see anyway, except that maybe there were lots more people either dead or grieving in the world.

All that jargon just didn't sink in and mean a thing. It went in one ear and out the other, and I never could keep any of it sorted out and straight. All those odd words and abbreviations were always getting jumbled up in my head so I really only had the slightest inkling of what it was that Gunar was trying to tell me in the letters that he sent home from the war. I never did get what all the ranks and positions were; who tells who what they should be doing, and how it all works together is still a mystery to me. But I know that it does work. Everybody in the world knows at least that much, I think.

When Gunar came home for that one precious week after boot camp, just before they shipped him off to Southeast Asia, I was shocked by just the sight of him. They had taken my boy, the one with the shaggy blond hair that I had always liked to let grow a bit too long, and they had turned him into someone else altogether. They had shaved his head and toughened him up so he was all muscle and military swagger. If it hadn't been for that birthmark of his, I might have thought that maybe they had made a mistake and sent me the wrong boy.

But then, when he came back home again a year and a half after that, it was even worse. We were all so relieved to see that he'd come though it unhurt—except for a funny round scar, the size of a half dollar, on his wrist that he said

119

had been left there by an infection of some kind, a "gook sore" was what he called it—it was a while before any of us even noticed how sleepless and on edge he'd become. And Gunar was so thin, thinner even than Bo ever did get, even at his worst when it all went bad. Gunar's bones just stuck right out and his eyes were sunk back in so deep and dark and full of bad secrets and his digestion was never working quite right besides, so it didn't matter what I fed him, he still stayed thin.

He had started to remind me of his father. His hair was darker. And he was so jumpy. He couldn't sit still, it seemed, and he couldn't sleep. A good clap of thunder was enough to send him on a run outside into the rain.

That's what they did. They ruined him.

He didn't care to talk about it.

Bo angered and embarrassed him by being proud.

"It's not a thing for pride," Gunar said, flushing up red and nasty at the tips of his ears. "Listen to me, Bo," and then he clamped his hand down so strong like a vice on Bo's shoulder and turned him around to look at him close and keen.

He pursed his lips up tight as if he were maybe going to blow a kiss, but that wasn't it at all. He frowned hard and shook his head and pushed Bo roughly away, and he turned and stomped out of the house as if he believed that he was the one who had just been hurt.

Bo, he had to laugh. He thought it was just Gunar being modest, the same way he'd been back when he was playing football and had taken a good tackle and then tried to shrug it off as if it were nothing unusual at all. Gunar, the Marine, the one who had been out there fighting for our freedom in a steamy, faraway jungle while Bo was home finishing up his high school years; Gunar coming back all gristle and bone and saying it wasn't a thing for pride. Bo would laugh and shake his own head and go out to find his big brother and fetch him home again.

It went on like that night after night, from the time that Gunar stepped off that bus. And then, finally, it all just came to a once-and-for-all-time stop. No more head shaking. No more stomping out the door. Gunar put an end to all of it, like that.

"It's not a thing for pride, Bo," he was saying over and over again. He could tell that Bo wasn't believing it, and that was what made him mad. "I'm not proud. I'm not brave. And I'm not a goddamn hero."

And Bo started to smile, looking back at him as if he knew better, and that tough, hard hand of Gunar's clamped down so tight on Bo's shoulder that I thought I could almost hear it click into place. I could see the tears well up into Bo's eyes.

Gunar's were so dark, but there was a gleam back in there, too, like one lone coal still lit up and smoldering hot as ever at the bottom of a burned-out fire.

"No," Gunar growled. "You're not going in. Not ever."

He knew what it was that Bo was thinking about doing. Bo was thinking how he would enlist, too, just like his big brother had done.

"Not ever," Gunar said again, and Bo's knees buckled under the force of Gunar's furious grip on his shoulder.

I could see that Bo was biting his lip and wincing and trying to be strong and brave. He nodded, quickly, though. "Never," he whispered, gasping and hoarse, his teeth bared and his lips pulled back. "Not ever."

And then Gunar let go and Bo fell down and curled up into a ball with his own hand crossed over onto his shoulder where Gunar's had been before, and all those tears and all that pain.

Gunar had, with his bare hand, broken Bo's collarbone. That was the click that I heard. The snapping of bone.

And Gunar was right, too. Bo had wanted to join up. He was only waiting for the best time, was all. He had had it planned all along. Gunar knew it. Bo wanted to be brave, too. He wanted to be a hero, and he wanted to be strong. But Gunar said no, and that was all that there would be to that.

And then Gunar who had said no went off to Omaha with Neva Jolene Boots and extended his tour while he was there. Nobody could believe it, not even Neva Jolene, but that was what he did. He said it just had to be that way. He told me—out back in the corner where I had the lilies coming up, with a handful of tender bulbs cupped so gentle in his palm, that same hard hand that had broken his own brother's collarbone and probably pulled the trigger on a few enemy soldiers, too—he said to me that he was just not the same person anymore.

In case I hadn't noticed.

He said to me that he didn't think that he could be doing anything else if he wasn't out fighting in that war. He was just waiting for it to finally be over. He said to me that he had friends he had left behind. It was as if he felt more at home out there in the bush than he ever could again on the streets of Wizen River. And he said that he would be promoted probably and get more money for it this time around, and that had to count for something, didn't it?

When I told him he was crazy, he said he guessed he probably was, and he smiled at me then.

So, that was it. Gunar went back to his war, which was his job. And then it was as if he was going for Bo, in Bo's place, wasn't it? What could Bo have done? If he went against the "not ever" that his brother had made him swear, then Gunar would be out there, risking his life like that, a second time, pushing his luck, for nothing at all.

So Bo stayed home. With me. And there wasn't Dr. Diettermann or my daddy around anymore to do a thing about it to make it any different from the way it was.

"Don't touch me," Gunar had said. "Don't look at me. Don't copy me. Don't do the things I do."

10

Dear Annie D.

COELUM NON ANIMUM MUTANT
QUI TRANS MARE CURRUNT

Nothing much comes to me through the mail these days. There used to be more, I think. The box still sits sentry out there at the end of the front walk—new bricks that I laid down myself that summer after the Doctor died, replacing the old limestone that had begun to chip and separate over the years of bad weather and wear. The box sports a jaunty cap of snow in winter, glazed over as if it were ceramic after one of our nights of freezing rain, twined up by midsummer in the jasmine that I've planted at its base.

These days it's become a receptacle for more throwaway mail than real correspondence. The only things in my mailbox that are of any interest are the bills, which don't amount to very much, but can't be ignored, either, and the catalogues that come in ever growing numbers—stacks and stacks of them from stores and mail-order houses in places like Maine and Texas and California and Rhode Island and New York.

There used to be more. There used to be notes from Phoebe. Even though my house was only a short drive down the hill from the Tooker Place, and we talked to each other

123

over the phone nearly every day anyway, she would still always be dropping in clippings of some interest from one of those magazines that she subscribed to, or recipes, or a reminder about a plan we maybe had for pickling the garden cukes or driving out to some farm for a look at the heirlooms and family treasures that they would be auctioning off because the last member of the family had finally died or the youngest one had mortgaged everything to the bank and then gone broke.

Phoebe wrote to me because she didn't have anybody else. She didn't even know then where Lacey was.

Or there would be the usual invitations to one thing or another: showers or weddings or christenings or birthday parties for the boys' friends. My mother's family wrote only once in a long, long while, and then it was only to say that one or another of them had married or divorced or remarried or had a child or lost a child or died. Mona never wrote to me at all.

But then, when the boys were grown up and Lacey Tooker went to California and Gunar had joined up again with the Marines, that was when all those letters really started to come in. I'd read a letter one time, then maybe carry it around in my purse or my pocket for a while, and read it again whenever I was missing one of those kids. Finally I would put it away in my top dresser drawer with the rest until my bundle there had enough bulk to be getting in the way. Then I would just throw the whole thing out altogether.

I should have taken them all up to the steamer trunk in the attic, where they could have been kept, tucked safely away in shoe boxes, tied together with string. If I had done that, I could sit in my garden and read them now. I should have kept them.

But I wasn't thinking then that they were going to be all that I had left.

It was in the spring of 1970 that Lacey Tooker went away. After Phoebe found out about Lacey being pregnant, and not, as she had hoped and he had dreamed, by Bo, I offered to help out by talking to Darla Williams about what they could maybe do. It was funny to think that Phoebe really believed there might be a way to work things out so Lacey's reputation wouldn't be soiled by what had been going on between her and that Boots boy ever since the summer night when they had caught each other's eye in Center Park. Because by then everybody who had eyes to see knew what was wrong with Lacey Tooker and why she was looking so plump and preoccupied all the time.

It was my own opinion that things would be best all around, in the long run, if not the short, if Lacey was to just stay put. There wasn't any good reason why she needed to be running off to hide in California.

But what about the baby? That was what Phoebe Tooker wanted to know. What were they supposed to do with it? And she rolled her eyes at the idea of an infant squalling around her house again, and an illegitimate one at that, and Casey Boots the father besides.

And what about Casey Boots? What if he decided to come forward and do the right thing by marrying Lacey?

And what about Lacey? Phoebe had always hoped and assumed that Lacey would finish up her high school and go on to college and marry well. Or, anyway, better than that.

It was too much for Phoebe to swallow and work out all at once. She was losing her patience quickly with me and all my ideas about what I thought she could and maybe should do. So, when she finally asked me to do it, I went ahead and spoke to Darla, and it happened that she did know of a place on the beach, or close to it anyway, in Los Angeles, that would take in a young, pregnant, unmarried girl—if anyone happened to know of one, that is, and I never once admitted outright that I did—and find a good home for the infant once it was born.

So that was how it went. On a recommendation from Darla Williams, with her wavy hair and her beauty mark, Phoebe sent Lacey out west to that home. The farther away from Casey Boots, the better, was how Phoebe put it to me when she stopped in on her way back from the bus station that morning when Lacey went away. The plan then was that Phoebe would fly out to be with her daughter when the time came in October.

Meanwhile, Casey Boots graduated from high school, and he took that job at the gas station, working there for Eddie Fly, who, because his eyes had begun to fog up on him, was ready to hand over some of the work, and who said that pumping gas and working on the engines ought to be a job good enough for any man, but who was only just saying so because it had been a job that he had never expected to be good enough for him.

I remember how hot it was that summer, because that old Chevy that Phoebe was still driving even way back then kept overheating and breaking down on her, and she kept having to take it in to get it fixed, and every time she did that, she would have to stop and talk to Casey Boots. She hated that.

I saw him, too, every time I needed gas for my own car, and he was always polite and glad to take care of my needs for me. He would wash not just the front windshield, but all the glass all the way around and the headlights, too, and he would fiddle with things under the hood, a greasy rag wrapped over his hand.

Phoebe complained because his hair was long, and she said that she thought he smelled pretty bad besides, but that was only sweat, to be expected because it really was awfully hot that summer, and grease, and if he looked dirty and unkempt, that was only because he was working in a garage. I could remember Harley when he came in from the barn where he had that old tractor gutted and its pieces everywhere because he was trying to get the darned thing running right again, and he looked and smelled a lot like Casey Boots. But, as I told Phoebe, that was only because of what their jobs were; it wasn't anything bad in them. I just had to wonder what kind of smells and dirt Jack Tooker brought home to Phoebe when he was still working in the pork department at the slaughterhouse.

Anyway, Casey was always nice and polite and all, and after I had been in a few times, he started in telling me about how he sure did miss having Lacey around, but he would keep on working the way he was until winter came, and then he'd be going out there to be with her, because she was saying in her letters about how she didn't much care anymore for the idea of coming back home to Nebraska now that she had seen how nice it was out where she was living now. But, well, he was going to have to save up some cash first, and that wasn't so easy a thing for him to do. Jack Tooker's money, what had come in from all that life insurance that he had bought and left behind for Lacey to collect on, wasn't going to last them forever.

And he sure was going to hate to have to leave his mom.

Casey would shrug and snap the gas cap back into place and wink at me as if we had some kind of an understanding that went back and forth just between the two of us. He said that he would wait around, working and saving, until it got cold in Wizen River, and then he would be heading out west to where it would still be warm enough to walk around in shirtsleeves and shorts.

Lacey's baby was due in the middle of October, so at the end of September, just when that false promise of Indian summer had begun to fade and cool down some, Phoebe took the bus to Omaha and flew from there to be with her daughter when the time came. Even Phoebe knew that it wasn't going to be an easy time for Lacey.

Phoebe was gone for only three full days, and then her telephone call came from the airport in Omaha to tell me that she was on her way back home again, and would I meet the bus and give her a lift up the hill to her house? Her voice was under such control over the phone; I could hear it strung up tight as the wires that connected us across the fields. I was afraid to ask any questions then, for fear she might lose the grip that she had on herself and fall apart before she had made it safe home again.

She did seem so tired and worn right down when she stepped off that bus. It looked to me as if she'd been crying, but it may have been sleeplessness and travel that left her face so pale and her eyes puffy and lined.

She was stiff-lipped and still holding on tight at first. And I knew enough to stay quiet and clammed up myself. When we got up to the house—the trees were turning and their warm colors must have been a truly welcome sight to her—and she was dragging her bags out of the car, I could tell just by how she wasn't looking at me that she was wishing I didn't know even as much as I did, that I was just a stranger who could be paid off and sent away.

But there must have been part of her that wanted me to stay and hear the story, too.

One half of her would have liked only to crawl into her bed and sleep it off, heavy and deep, and the other half longed to get it off her chest and tell her best friend and most constant sympathizer all about what had gone on between herself and her willful daughter in the last three days. So, torn between the two, she dropped the bags there in the drive and plopped herself down on the front step and stretched out her legs so her shoes fell off into the grass.

Her feet were swollen, and there were red lines on the insteps where her shoes had pinched them. She patted the place next to her for me to sit, too.

California was just an awful place, she said. "Hideous. Infernal. Wicked. And mean."

There was so much sun, and the light had burned into her eyes, and it gave her headaches that were worse than anything that she had ever suffered here before. In the afternoon, when the sun was at its most merciless peak, she would have to creep back to her room at the motel and pull the blinds and turn on the air and just lie down there in the dark until the sun had finally set over the water.

Phoebe was picking at the paint on the porch step while she talked, snapping it off in little chips that clung stubbornly to her fingertips. "Too many people," she said. "Too many cars." The air was too hot and too dirty to breathe.

She sighed and picked, until her palm was flecked with white and there was a big gray splotch there on the step where the wood showed through.

But there was more than just the sun and the people and the cars and the smog. There was Lacey, too. They had argued, Phoebe said. Not just another one of their small disagreements this time around. There had been enough of those over the years, God knew. But now, well, it looked as if maybe this time this was going to be it. The last straw, Phoebe said. And here she stopped talking and sighing and picking at the paint, and she leaned against me, and she wept.

We sat together, there on the porch steps, and I patted her and rocked her just as if she were the child herself. Finally I was able to get her onto her feet again and into the house and up to bed all tucked in cool and cozy, with the shades drawn and an aspirin and some warm milk with a touch of bourbon to sweeten and soothe. But Phoebe kept right on talking through all of that; it was as if once she had let go that hold and got it all started, she just couldn't find a way to get it to stop again.

She talked about the home Lacey was in, the ugly lime-green rooms that they had tried to cheer up with Indian prints and big, shaggy pillows. The sallow-faced girls with their hanging breasts and full bellies, and all that sunshine burning down and bringing out the worst of everything. Rain would have been better, she said. A cloudy day would have made it easier to take. The sun was just too bright and unforgiving; there was no place to hide anything at all under its glare.

I thought how it was just like somebody from Nebraska to blame the whole thing on the weather.

And then finally, Phoebe said, as if everything wasn't enough already to drive a loving and concerned mother crazy and out of her mind, Lacey had gone and turned on her.

"I plan to keep this baby," was what Lacey had said, with her hands on her belly as if it were a big beach ball that some other kid was threatening to snatch away. "I won't give it up. Not to anyone. I don't care who."

And those social workers, who were always smiling so nice and calling everybody "dear," with their noses pushed up against everybody else's business and they called that doing their job—they were supposed to be helping, weren't they? that was what they were being paid for, wasn't it?—had sided with Lacey against her mother, right down the line, all the way. She was eighteen—though really only just—and that was old enough, they said. A woman has some rights, they told Phoebe. A woman's body, and everything in it, belongs, ultimately, to nobody else but her.

Then, when Phoebe had only been trying to reason with Lacey, because she loved her and really only wanted what would be best for her, Lacey had turned vicious and started in with all her nasty, wicked accusations.

"Where did they come from?" Phoebe asked me, sitting up in bed, tissues crumpled in her fists. "Why?"

Phoebe couldn't even bring herself to repeat any of them for me just then. Later she did, of course, many times, more than I ever wanted to hear. About how Lacey said that Phoebe was so selfish and so weak and was always putting her own interests ahead of everybody else's; about how Phoebe had never even really liked her own daughter very much, or her husband either—she had only married him to get her father's attention, and when that didn't work, well, it just made everything else that much worse, didn't it? About how Phoebe really seemed to enjoy her own unhappiness and disappointment with the way that her life had turned out, maybe even invented some of the things, thrived on them, in fact, and on and on like that. Cruel things, doubly vicious in the half truth of their invention.

So that was it. Phoebe had no choice but to pack up and come home. She couldn't have stood it for one more day. First her husband had betrayed her, and now her daughter was turning her back on her, too. Was she such a mean and terrible person that she deserved to be treated this badly? she asked, snuffling noisily and sopping up the damp with another fat wad of pink tissue from the flowered box on the table by the bed.

"No," I said. "There, there now. No, of course you're not mean, and you're not terrible either."

I never said she wasn't selfish.

Phoebe had only wanted some attention. Lacey had been on the button about that, I thought. But she went about getting it for herself in such a way that made her so unlikable that it was, well, hard to really love her very much. That didn't mean Lacey was right to be so mean. It didn't give her the freedom to go ahead and be so cruel. To her own mother.

"There, there," I said. "Don't cry. Drink this. Close your eyes. Get some sleep."

Phoebe took another sip of her bourbon and milk, and I gently nudged her down off her elbows and onto her back so that her head was nestled in the soft pillow, and she held my hand and closed her red, swollen eyes, and her face, which had been all squinched up with grief and misery, went slack so that her lips bubbled a little as she slept, snoring so quietly that it was almost like a purr.

Lacey and Phoebe Tooker never spoke to each other again after that. They never wrote or sent any pictures. And Lacey didn't come back to Wizen River until after Phoebe was dead.

She did send letters to me, though. *Dear Annie D.*, she would write. And pictures of the baby, too—as an infant and then a toddler and then a schoolboy.

I never showed any of them to Phoebe. I really didn't believe that she would ever want to know.

Dear Annie D., Lacey wrote.

The first letter came just after Phoebe's sudden return home to Wizen River. Lacey wasn't happy with how it had all ended up, but she wasn't sorry enough to give up any of the ground she felt she'd gained. She was going to have that

131

baby, and then she was going to keep it for her own and raise it up herself. She would show her own mother how it was supposed to be done.

She had been in California for almost five months already by then, and that was long enough for her to learn that it was different, and better, too, to be living with people who didn't already know all that there was to know about Lacey Tooker. People who couldn't make assumptions or jump to conclusions based on anything that they had seen or heard about years before. People who treated her with interest, and respect.

And she wasn't going to say she was sorry for anything that she had ever done with Casey Boots, either. She wasn't ashamed. It wasn't ugly and it wasn't bad, because she truly loved Casey, and Casey truly loved her right back.

She said that there was sure nothing wrong with the fact that she was pregnant. Okay, maybe the timing wasn't exactly right, maybe it had happened a little bit sooner than it should, but it wasn't some shameful disease that she was suffering from. And that was just the way her mother had been looking at it.

But there was a baby in there, for heaven's sake. Not some crazy conglomeration of cells with hair and teeth. And Lacey Tooker was sure enough the baby's mother, and so she would have to have it and love it just like all the rest of us had had and loved our own babies. Wasn't that fair? She had tried to explain this to Phoebe, but Phoebe only heard what she wanted to hear.

So enough is enough, Lacey wrote.

Casey had been in touch with her to say that he was working for Eddie Fly and that he saw me now and then at the pumps. And how he was saving up the money that he made and would be out there to take care of Lacey and the baby very soon. When he got there, she said, they could be a real family, the three of them.

And then, two weeks later, another letter from Lacey. *Dear Annie D.*

She told me that she had had a boy, after a miserably long

132

and drawn-out labor that had ended in an emergency Caesarean section, and she had named him John Tooker after his grandfather, her daddy, and wouldn't Jack have wished that he could be around for that? She said that the baby John had dark hair and blue eyes, just like Casey, and that he was handsome, too. She was back at the home, recovering, but would be moving out and into a place of her own soon to make room there for some other girl who had found herself in trouble.

I went in for gas again soon after that letter came, and Casey was still there, looking skittish and afraid now. He was always glancing up at the sky, as if maybe he was expecting some sudden change in the weather, keeping a watch out for the winter that would be coming soon to send him west to be with his new family. He seemed a little dirtier and his hair really was getting too long—it was straight and shaggy-looking, and gone was the baby hair that had curled so prettily around his ears so many years before. He looked to me like he was losing weight and getting thin.

I told him how happy I had been to get word from Lacey about the baby, but he didn't seem to be hearing my words. He just kept looking up at the sky, and he didn't give me his usual smile and wink when he was finished with the gas.

"She said she's going to keep it," Casey said. "She's not going to give it away."

That news about John must have really overwhelmed him. The responsibility must have seemed immense. And he had begun to smell a little sour, I thought.

Not long after that, Mrs. Boots came in to clean for me, but instead of slipping in through the back onto the service porch where all the rags and sponges and soaps and polishes were kept, she came right up to the front door and rang the bell. And instead of going on out to the kitchen to get to her work, which began with the dishes and ended with the floors, she walked right through the hall and into the living room and, without so much as a "Good morning, Annie

D.," she sat herself right down there in the big chair by the fireplace. And I just tagged along in after her, as if this was what we always did, though it was not.

She looked around the room, at my plants and my books and the curios on the mantel, finally letting her shining eyes meet mine, sizing me up, it seemed, though more likely she was just trying very hard to find the best way to begin whatever it was that she was about to say.

"Not too dirty today," was what she came up with, settling back into the chair with her big, bony hands folded and intertwined like tree roots in her lap.

She was right, it wasn't. With Gunar gone, we were hardly using much more of the house than the sitting room and the kitchen and the bedrooms and bath. The examining rooms and the Doctor's office had been closed up already for years.

I could easily have kept my house clean for myself, but I just hadn't had the heart, or the nerve, either, to let Mrs. Boots go. She had so desperately wanted the job and needed the money in the beginning. And she had been so determined to convince me to take her on.

And now, here she was, quitting.

"I gotta quit, Annie D.," she said. Just as if it hadn't been her idea to come to work here for me in the first place. I didn't know whether to be relieved or afraid.

Mrs. Boots was sitting there in that chair smiling so her big teeth gleamed, with her hands in her lap and rubbing her knuckles with her broad, flat thumbs.

"It's the arthritis, you know," she said, and she winced, just to show me it was real. "And, well, you've always been so good to us, Annie D., and, well, there's that old bookstore what's been shut up for so long, and, well, my Casey, he's been talking about it. Dreaming, I guess you'd have to say."

That morning was the first I heard about the old bookstore that Casey Boots had been looking to turn into a sort of café. He had it all planned out, his mother said. He'd make it a place where all the kids could go, with food and music,

134

dancing, and maybe even a pinball machine or two. Now it was only a matter of money, and that was where I was supposed to come in. With the cash in hand.

"Really it was Neva Jolene's idea, but Casey . . . well, I guess you know what it means to want to make your child's dreams come true," she said. "I always only wanted them to have the same thing any other mother wants. You understand that."

I told her that of course I did.

"Not to mention all what's been going on and on about that girl Lacey Tooker, too," Mrs. Boots continued. She leaned forward and shook her head at me. "She said she's going to keep the baby. He doesn't want to go to her, you know."

I didn't know that. It was news to me.

"I haven't been pushing him, if that's what you think," Mrs. Boots said. "I haven't said anything one way or the other about it." She shrugged. "But Casey's a good boy. You know that. And whatever he decides to do, it'll be the right thing."

She had been smiling, but here she frowned and winced again, and it really was the pain this time, I could tell, because her boy was in trouble. It was only for a minute, a brief shadow, and then she was smiling and going on again about how interest was just so high at the bank and maybe they wouldn't want to give her the money anyway, and it would just be sort of a loan with me, of course. They would pay it all back, and then some, too.

"Consider it an investment," Mrs. Boots said. "An investment, not a favor. Or a loan."

All this time I had been standing, as if this were her home and not mine, and I was the guest, and then she put out her rough and calloused hand to offer me a chair, to tell me to sit down.

"A person shouldn't have to make a big decision like this standing up," she said.

I didn't sit down, though. I didn't make myself comfortable. I stayed where I was, and I told her that I would have to think about what she had said. I would let her know, and soon, because I understood that time was short. I told her that she really didn't need to stay and clean today, because, as she had already pointed out for me herself, the house wasn't very dirty at all.

She stood up, a head taller than I was so I had to tip back to see her clearly, and said thank you and gathered up her things and walked back home again.

In the end, I did say yes to Casey.

He came by himself a few days later, with his hair cut and his face clean and his clothes all buttoned up and tucked in where they should be. I told him that he would have a fine business if he worked hard at it. He said that a man can't be pumping gas all his life, now can he?

And he winked at me when he said it, because he knew that I would understand all that he was saying by it even though neither of us had mentioned either Lacey or baby John. He promised me that he was going to make a good business of it, that he'd bring in a profit, and that some of it would be mine.

It was all arranged. Casey borrowed the cash from me, and he bought the bookstore, and he and Neva Jolene went in together to fix it up. Mrs. Boots, when all the papers had been signed and everything was official, took me in her big arms and nearly crushed me with her gratitude before she went home to tend to her own housekeeping instead of mine.

Dear Annie D.

Lacey's letter wasn't long in coming. Casey had let her know that he wouldn't be joining her out in California after all. That now he had a business of his own in Wizen River, and he wouldn't be able to get away. He asked her to come back here with the baby, if she wanted to, but he must have known she never would. She wouldn't go home to her mother. Lacey Tooker maybe loved Casey Boots a lot. But she hated her mother even more.

She had an apartment then, and a job, too, and she and John were happy where they were. Her neighbors all called her Mrs. Tooker, and they thought that she had a husband who was missing in action in Vietnam.

I guess it's probably true that I've never really been what you would call in love. That all-consuming passion that other people talk and write about hasn't ever been fanned into flame for me. I was the Doctor's wife for seventeen years, and we got along well enough. We didn't argue over anything much, and we were good to each other, and careful and kind. But I don't believe that I ever really loved him.

Not like Jack Tooker loved Phoebe Wink.

Not the way that Lacey Tooker loved that Casey Boots.

When I told Bo all about it, what had happened, with the bookstore and Casey staying here, I could tell by the way he smiled that he was glad.

So, maybe I did it for him. He is my son. My loyalties have always been straightforward. Whose side I was on has always been crystal clear.

Or maybe I just didn't know. Maybe I figured that it really didn't matter who Lacey loved, that she could love one just as well as another if she just would put her heart into it. And as long as her loving that Casey Boots was getting everybody else so upset and unhappy, well, maybe it would be better all around if she had a good reason not to anymore.

Like that he didn't love her back.

137

11

The Truth About Gunar

DULCE ET DECORUM EST
PRO PATRIA MORI

Even though I'd been the Doctor's wife for seventeen years, and, during that time, had seen enough of his patients coming and going every day and even heard firsthand accounts with much medical detail included about how one or the other of them had given in and died, either peacefully or thrashing out and fighting against it all the way, I never saw a dead person for myself except two times. One of them was the Doctor, who by then had so wasted away with cancer that he looked as good as dead even when he was still alive, and the other was a stranger that I saw just for a moment, from far away, passing by.

The Doctor and I had left the boys at home with Mrs. Boots to drive out along the highway south of town to try a new restaurant that Phoebe had read about in one of her magazines in an article about little-known and out-of-the-way eating places for anyone who happened to be driving the interstate across the middle of the country on his way to someplace else. They served authentic German food, home-cooked and brought to the table family style. I remember the Doctor thought that it was very good, except he commented later that the gravy was thin and the sausage tough.

I was happy to be going anywhere at all, feeling freed from the boys, on my own and able to relax with the Doctor, talk and have a complete conversation if we wanted, uninterrupted by Gunar's endless questions and Bo's noisy play.

There was this station wagon plodding along in front of us for the first half of the way there, going much too slowly, the Doctor complained, even though the roads were slick with a skim of wet snow that had come down and stuck that afternoon. It wasn't quite dark yet, but the snow had stopped, and so I had a good clear view of the young girl who was sitting cross-legged, riding backward in the wagon up ahead.

She had smooth, white skin and thick, yellow hair that fluffed out around her face, and I'm sure her eyes must have been blue. Like china plates. She looked so sweet, and happy, too. She was admiring the sky, which was pink with the sunset and the clouds and the new snow on the fields. Overhead, a flock of geese was soaring resolutely south. The girl was wearing a parka and a muffler and smiling so she looked like she might be humming some contented little song to herself.

And then we heard the sirens up ahead and saw the lights that flashed red and yellow and blue arcs across the snow, and I looked away from the girl as we slowed down to get around what appeared to be a pretty serious wreck. A blue pickup truck had skidded off the road and down the embankment, and when I craned to see, there she was, a woman not much older than Mrs. Boots, and very like her, so that I thought for just a second that it was her, but it wasn't, of course, she was home with Gunar and Bo. This other woman was hanging out through the shattered front windshield with her cheek resting ever so gently on the hood so that she faced up toward the road above and the sky and the clouds and the geese.

I saw more than I ever wanted to see. The shards of glass

that might have been ice shining in her hair. The one bigger chunk in her forehead—a triangle of glass stuck there with just a trickle of blood at its base. The pale skin, white as snow. The open mouth. The glassy, blind eyes, black with death. I wondered if we should maybe stop, but then we were already past and the Doctor said that there sure wasn't going to be anything for him to do there anyway.

"She's vay gone out of my reach by now, Annie," he said, touching my arm. "Can't do one thing to heal vat's already dead."

He was hungry, and he was anxious to get to his bratwurst and sauerkraut.

When I turned around and looked back up at the little girl in the car ahead of us, the one who had been so calm and so pretty and so untroubled only seconds before, I could tell that she must have had a good view of that dead woman, too. Just the sight had turned her ugly, with her face all red and wrenched up and distorted by her horror. She had her little fist rammed into her mouth and her eyes were wild and wide, and then she disappeared into the front of the car.

That's what death does. It takes you by surprise; just when you're not looking, when you think that things are all right, it comes along and takes what was beautiful and dear and turns it into something ugly and crazy and mean.

I always felt a lot safer when the Doctor was still around to take care of us. He was there when Gunar cut his finger on the scalpel and when Bo cracked his head on the table. He could get them both to do things that neither of them would ever agree to do for me. He could come between them and settle any argument or let it go into a fistfight with bloody noses and split lips and still be sure that things didn't get too far out of hand.

I could only worry. I imagined disasters all the time. When they were little, it was that the babies might stop breathing in their sleep or swallow poison or drown. I woke up sweating from dreams of Gunar falling out of the car on the highway, then bouncing around on the bone-breaking pavement as I drove away, unaware. With Bo the nightmare was that I had left him in the tub alone just long enough to get a clean towel and then something would distract me and something else and something else and by the time I finally did get back to him it was way too late and he was already floating, face down in the gray water, gone.

Then, when they got older, it was car accidents, drugs, diseases, and, finally, war.

The man who came to tell me about Gunar introduced himself as Major Petrick. It was in the springtime, April 24th, 1972, and it was raining, and on the TV and the radio they had been predicting hail. I was so worried about my bulbs—the ones that Gunar himself had helped me plant and that were just beginning to send up their shoots out back in the garden—and what damage a good hailstorm might do to them. As it turned out it didn't hail at all that night, and the garden was just fine, except for what I did to the bulbs myself the next day.

This is the part that I don't want to tell.

He was a major, he said, but that didn't mean a thing to me. He had driven all the way out from Lincoln to my house. He had news, he said. The car out on the street was mud-spattered and green. Could he come in? Would I like to sit down? Major Petrick was a short, solid man who perspired a lot, or maybe that was only the rain that had him all soaked and dripping and mopping his brow. He was in his uniform, but he didn't look as smart as he probably should have. I remember I noticed that he had mud on his shoes. I remember how surprised I was to find him standing there at the door like that, with his hat in his hands.

I should have been able to guess why he was there.

But I just kept getting so distracted by the rain and wondering whether it was going to turn to hail or not. I couldn't concentrate. I couldn't keep my mind on what it was he had to say. I kept listening for that first ping of ice on the windowpane, even after Major Petrick had stepped

141

inside and made me sit down and handed me the papers and told me all of that about my Gunar.

And how he was dead.

He was killed by enemy fire, the major said. He died a hero's death. KIA, they called it. Killed in Action. His body would be back in Wizen River again soon.

I kept smiling at the major, and then I would think that I had heard a ping and I would have to go to the window to see, but it was still only rain coming down in sheets where the front porch light shone through it, and the major didn't seem to know or even care very much about whether it would hail or not, but he was trying to tell me that Gunar, my Gunar, lank and blond with a birthmark on his chest small enough to fit under my thumb, one just like the scar my daddy, his grandfather, had—Gunar Diettermann, my son, no mistake, who was supposed to outlive his mother by years and years and years, was gone. Dead.

Bo was standing on the stairs, and he heard everything that Major Petrick was saying. His face was pasty white with the shock of it. He tried to grab Major Petrick, as if he would kill him, but the major was strong, and fast, and he took hold of Bo and held him down until he stopped screaming and just lay still, with his mouth hanging open and his eyes empty and drool bubbling on his lips. I don't know who called her or how, but pretty soon Darla Williams was all of a sudden there in the living room, telling me that, she didn't think, no, there wouldn't be any hail tonight, and anyway she was right about that.

But Gunar was dead.

They took Bo up to his room and gave him a shot of something to calm him down. He'll be all right, they told me. It was the shock of it. He'll get over it. He'll be fine. Father Phil was there, with one hand on my shoulder, and Mrs. Boots and Phoebe Tooker, too.

Then Darla made me take some pills, and I went to sleep, but I couldn't help it, I was lying there in the bed and I wasn't thinking about Gunar, or Bo either; I was worried about my bulbs, and I was still listening for the ping of that first chunk of hail against the glass.

It was Neva Jolene Boots's face that I woke up to when I opened my eyes again the next morning. Her head was turned so that the bad half of her face was hidden, like the dark side of the moon, and what I saw in that young profile of hers was real beauty that outmatched even a face like Lacey Tooker's. Her dark hair curled against her cheek and then up around her head, and it seemed to glow just like a halo there. Of course, that aura of hers was really only a trick of the midmorning light that was pouring in so bright through the curtains behind her. She was sitting there in the chair by the window, the one with all the black and ragged cigarette burns on its arms, where the Doctor had spent so many nights when his sleep was stolen from him by his bad memories and dreams.

My first thoughts were wondering how long Neva Jolene had been sitting there, watching me and waiting for me to wake up. What would she be doing?

And then I remembered about the hail. I threw myself up out of the bed and hurried over to the window to see, but the garden didn't look damaged the way it would have if it had been hit by hail. Only the rain that left the world wet and warm and the tree trunks black and everything else so green that it made my eyes ache in my head to see.

And then was when it all came back to me, in a rush, a flood, a painful, drenching wave of realization and grief about that man, the major, and Gunar, and that had to be the reason why Neva Jolene Boots with her ruined face was there, in my house, in my room, in the Doctor's chair. Before she had a chance to say one thing, or even try to stop me, I was on my way downstairs and through the kitchen where Mrs. Boots sat chewing on a sweet role and reading my newspaper. Already there were casseroles and baked goods, Jell-O and finger sandwiches, piled up in plastic containers and plates covered with plastic wrap and alumi-

143

num foil all around on the counters. That's how quickly the news had spread.

I banged on out through the back screen door to the garden and pulled up with my bare hands all those bulbs that I had worried over. The same ones that Gunar had helped me put in the last time that I saw him, so many months before. The rain had turned everything into black mud, and it stuck—on my nightgown and my hands, under my nails and in between my toes, in my mouth and in my hair—and I tore up all those bulbs and flung the mud around me every which way, and then I collapsed and pressed my face down hard into the muck.

The smell was so strong; I wanted to disappear, to suffocate myself, gag and strangle on the earth.

But Neva Jolene caught up with me, and she hoisted me up by my shoulders and pushed me back with so much fury that she tore my nightgown, and I was on my knees.

And how I must have looked, a raving mud-woman.

I could see Neva Jolene's whole face again then, and it wasn't so pretty anymore. She was staring right through me, and screaming, "No! No! Stop it! Stop!" and she drew back her hand as if she would slap me, but she didn't. She caught her hair back behind her ear. She leaned against me, so close that I could feel the hot steam of her breath against my face, and she whispered, "It's what he wanted. He's a hero now, Annie D."

"What?" The mud was gritty in my teeth.

"Gunar's a hero! That's what!" Tears filled her eyes and spilled over, running rivers down the purple, stained surface of her one cheek.

And that was when I figured it out that Neva Jolene Boots had loved my older son almost as dearly as I had myself.

Mrs. Boots had come out of the house by then, and she had her hands on her hips and was shaking her head and clucking in disapproval over what a big mess I had made of my garden and myself. She took me into the house and ran a bath for me, and when I came back downstairs, clean and fresh again, she and Neva Jolene and Bo were all waiting for me at the kitchen table.

What we had to do, they were saying, was make sure that the rest of Wizen River knew what a hero their own Gunar Diettermann had been. Nobody was ever gonna forget, Neva Jolene said, pounding the table with her fist. He gave his life to the cause of democracy; he went to war and died fighting communism so that the rest of us would be free to go our own way and pursue our own happiness.

Bo just sat there, staring at his hands.

A Marine Corps prop plane brought Gunar's casket in from Omaha late in the afternoon a few days later. They landed it out in one of the cornfields that had just been plowed up and was as wet with the rain as my garden had been. We all stood out there up to our ankles in the mud, and the high school band came and played some music that was mostly just carried off and lost in the wind. Then we trudged back to the cars, and Gunar's flag-covered casket was put into the hearse, and we snaked through town in one long slow line to the cemetery. They lowered Gunar's flag-covered casket down into the ground next to the body of his father, who had lost enough relatives to war already, I thought.

After it was all over, Neva Jolene drove me and Bo home. I don't know how many people spent the rest of that evening in their living rooms and their kitchens raising up their eyebrows at the idea of the three of us driving off together like that—it must have been an unlikely sight. I'm sure Phoebe Tooker had plenty to say about the situation herself, and probably she found people who would listen to what she thought. But Neva Jolene, just as her mother had been for many years already, was so much in charge of me and of herself, too, that it seemed only right for us to be together after all that had happened since Major Petrick had rung my doorbell on the night when it didn't hail.

That Neva Jolene had had her heart wrapped up in some sweet way with Gunar was clear. I never heard him say one thing at all about how he felt about her, but he wouldn't been at ease telling me that anyway. Now I thought I could pretty well guess just where it was he had always been going off to every night during the time when he was at home between his tours of duty in Vietnam. He must have thought I would have disapproved.

We drove back to my house after the funeral, and the more I looked at her, the less offensive Neva Jolene's birthmark seemed to be. I was guessing that maybe that was just how Gunar had been able to look at her, too. We pulled into the drive, and she grinned and brought out from behind the seat a big, fat, cold bottle of cheap white wine and three plastic glasses. Bo and I followed along through the gate and back into the garden. We all sat together, shoulder to shoulder there on the bench. She unscrewed the cap and poured the three glasses full and passed them around. And although it wasn't something that I had ever done before, I drank mine right down without even thinking.

"Gunar was a good man," Neva Jolene said, solemn and clear, refilling her glass again.

Bo was grinning and grimacing in a way that reminded me of that old tintype of Weary Shires. He raised his glass. "To the memory of Gunar Diettermann," he said. He gasped and then tipped his head back to pour the wine down his throat. His Adam's apple bobbed as he swallowed, gurgling.

"He was gentle," Neva Jolene said. "And kind."

I held out my empty glass, and Neva Jolene filled it to the top again.

"It should have been me," Bo said quietly, holding his cup in his lap, his head bowed down, chin buried in his chest. His shoulders shook. In cold weather, and when it rains, that collarbone of his will ache and ache. "Woulda been . . ."

"He took care of me," said Neva Jolene. "Nobody else in the world ever did a thing as nice as that." She laughed. "Except for him, nobody else thought there was anything about me that had a value worth bothering for."

146

Her laugh was as bitter and cold as the wine.

Gunar had always been such a frowning, serious boy, and so aware of what his duties in this world were. He had loved it when the Doctor was away for a night with a patient in Omaha and Gunar got to be in charge—the little gentleman, the man of the house.

"He was so serious," I said. "Things mattered to him. They were important. I remember when—"

"Duty," said Bo.

"Honor," I said.

"Love," said Neva Jolene.

Then I drank some more wine and so did Neva Jolene and so did Bo, and we talked some more and drank some more, and I was getting tipsy and then I was downright drunk. Neva Jolene let me touch her birthmark. She took my hand and pressed my palm up against her face and held it there, like it was a charm, a talisman, for wishes and for luck. I told her about Gunar's small white mark on his chest.

"I know," she said, closing her eyes. "I've seen it. I've touched it." She looked at me. "I've kissed it," she said. "I've licked it . . ."

"My father," I told her, "he had a scar there, in the same place, exactly like it, bigger."

Bo was bent over, with his face buried in his hands. He rocked against his knees, and moaned. Neva Jolene reached over and pulled him up to his feet and held him hard against her, whispering, "Poor Bo and poor Neva Jolene and poor Gunar and poor old Annie D."

"Shoulda been me," Bo said, his face twisted with the pain of it. "Woulda been . . ."

Until finally the wine was all gone and we fell down into the flowerbeds and went to sleep there in the moonlight under the trees.

That was how Phoebe Tooker found us the next morning. And she wasn't all that glad about it, either. She kicked Neva Jolene awake and prodded me and Bo not too much more gently and then shooed the girl away with insults and nasty accusations that Neva Jolene had probably heard before, because she didn't take it too hard at all, but only backed off and smiled and said thank you and good-bye to me and Bo and see you later and all of that.

Phoebe really did do her best. She was trying very hard. Now that she had finally got rid of all those Boots people, she meant to take over as my best friend, with all the sympathy that she could muster for what had happened to Gunar. She made coffee and poured orange juice. She cooked eggs for Bo, but he wouldn't eat. She was only meaning to do for me what I had done for her when she had lost Lacey, but it wasn't the same at all, because Lacey was still alive, and I would rather have had Gunar despise me than be dead and gone the way he was.

So what happened was that eventually it got turned around to where Phoebe was doing all the crying and I was doing all the shushing, and I think that maybe we were both just more comfortable with it that way.

"Oh, Annie D.," she said, her eyes wide, blue pools of sorrow and grief, "this whole world is just too darned sad for me."

I patted her shoulder. "There, there," I said. "It's really not so bad, Phoebe. It's really not so bad."

And I was so involved with her that I forgot about Bo, who had wandered off upstairs alone.

And it wasn't until the killing blast of gunshot thundered through the house that I remembered.

But by then it was too late.

Bo took his father's old gun, and he held it pressed up tight under his chin, and he squeezed the trigger.

"It should have been me," he had said. "Woulda been . . ."

I've thought and thought about this. And the only explanation I can come up with, the only one that makes sense is that Bo would just plain rather have been dead himself than to know his brother was gone. It was something that he knew he was not going to be able to bear. He had it

148

in his mind that it was somehow his own fault, and this was the thought that broke him. It took away whatever it was that kept him going. There was too much pain, and he couldn't take it. He couldn't stand it.

The bullet coursed up through the roof of his mouth and into his brain and out the back of his head, where it tore through the plaster and buried itself in a beam in the wall behind his bed.

It didn't kill him. Probably that was worse. There was more blood than I ever want to see again in this world, but the ambulance came, and he did not die. Might as well have, though, because it did somehow take him away. It damaged him forever. Or anyway what it left behind never again would be the same. Bo was gone forever after that.

Sometimes things happen that are just too terrible to stand, and that was how it was for Bo. He couldn't take the truth that Gunar was dead. He hated it that his brother had been killed. He tried his best to disappear, but it didn't work that way for him. He wasn't able to kill himself the way he wanted to.

But he did manage to get rid of the part of him that cared.

The doctors in Omaha brought Bo back, half of what he had been, if even that. Thin, white scars crisscrossed his throat. The back of his head was hairless and lumpy, so he wore a green baseball cap to keep it covered up.

We gave him a job, working as the park keeper in Center Park. He had lost weight, and he couldn't remember much of anything, but he was alive.

He loved his work, outside, in the air. He picked up trash in the summer, and mowed and kept the bushes trimmed. He planted the flowerbeds and weeded and watered. In the fall, he cleared away the leaves from the oaks and elms and maples that shaded the park. And in winter, he shoveled snow.

He was dreamy and easily lost track. He would stop what he was doing to lean on his rake and stare at the cold, blue sky. Or sit back on his haunches with the dirt and grass stains on his knees and gaze at the flowers in his hands. He would romp with the babies and laugh with the old men in the park. Run with the dogs.

I thought then that maybe he would get better. I thought that maybe time would heal. I was only glad he had survived. He was alive, and that was something. I would keep him that way. It could not be that both my sons would die before me. It was impossible that I could lose my boys. It would be too much. Everybody thought so.

And by the time Lacey Tucker and her son came back to Wizen River, we were all used to Bo being the way he was, like a little boy, trapped, who would never grow up. And for me, that was plenty.

It just had to be enough.

It was a year after we had turned Gunar into a hero and laid his lanky body to rest beside his father's in the plot at the Wizen River cemetery that Lance Corporal Neeley showed up like a hungry old cur on my front doorstep. He was a big, muscular man who had not in any way been thinned down and wasted away by the war the way Gunar was. If anything, Ted Neeley was just a few pounds overweight. His hunger wasn't in his belly, but in his heart and in his eyes. He didn't look to me, except maybe for that twitchy eagerness in his face, as though he had been off to any kind of a war at all. He was rosy and beefy, and he had smooth, pink cheeks and sandy hair cropped so short you could almost see the skin on his scalp. His pale, hazel eyes were set close together on that broad, fair face—as smooth and flat as a dinner plate—and sometimes when he set his gaze just so, you could swear that he was looking at you cross-wise.

He seemed pretty sure about who I was when we met. He had this small, sweet smile that he kept showing me, just to let me know that he knew all about everything I could possibly have to tell him. He introduced himself as "Lance Corporal Neeley, ma'am," even though he wasn't in the service anymore, and he wrapped his big hand around mine.

He said that he had been one of the members of Gunar's squad and even though I had maybe never heard of him, he sure had heard about me. Maybe he had really only known Gunar for what some people might think was a short time, but, well, combat has a way of speeding things up and pressing them in, and so he and Gunar had gotten to be pretty close out there in the bush together.

"Like that," he said, holding up two long, broad fingers and crossing them over each other. I remember that I noticed then how his nails were smooth and flat and clipped straight across, clean like that.

Close, except that he never had called him Gunar the way we did. What he said was the Dodger or the Dodge or just Dodger. He said they all called Gunar that because "he was just so goddamned good at dodging all that gooner frag."

Sometimes, plenty of times, I had no idea at all what it was Ted Neeley was talking to me about.

I didn't keep him standing like that on the doorstep while he told me those things. I asked him in, and he thanked me and came on in, and all the time he kept pursing up his lips into this funny, odd little smile and acting as if he had been here before or something and already knew all about anything I had to tell him. He said that was just because the Dodge had told him so much about Wizen River that it was a funny thing, but, well, Ted really did feel like maybe he had been here before. Which, of course, he hadn't.

Ted seemed to know plenty, though, about what had gone on here while Gunar was growing up. He had heard about that one winter when a terrible ice storm came in and froze all the power lines—so nobody had any electricity or phones—and at the same time turned the whole town into one big ice skating rink. He told me about the summer when Gunar and Bo put up the treehouse back in Tooker's woods and about the tornado that came along the next spring to blow it all back down again.

He even knew all there was to know about Lacey's dog Blue.

Gunar had shown him the thin, white scar on his finger

where I had by mistake gashed him with the Doctor's scalpel. Ted even knew about the photograph of myself and the Doctor that had hung up there on the wall of Gunar's bedroom and, rather than serve as a comfort to a small boy who imagined elephants lurking in the shadows, had always made Gunar feel that he didn't have any secrets he could keep from those two parents who were always there, watching, even in the dark, even when the door was closed.

Sure, Ted told me, the Dodger had talked about me, too. And how I liked to work in the yard so much—have my hands in the dirt was how he put it—and that's why I had by far the most beautiful flower gardens for miles and miles around. And then Ted looked quickly over his shoulder and lowered his voice and laid his big hand alongside his nose and said that Gunar had even told him about that time in the Doctor's office with, you know, Neva Jolene Boots. And then he was grinning and shrugging and crossing his eyes at me. That first time it happened, I thought that he was doing it on purpose.

Ted sighed with a big whoosh that puffed out his cheeks, and he looked around and wriggled a little on my sofa to get his big body comfortable there. He said that it was just such a shame. About Dodge, he meant.

"He was just like any of us, I guess. Just another one of them dumb kids who thought maybe he'd like to join up and see the sights."

He hoped I wouldn't take any offense. He wasn't meaning to imply that Gunar was stupid or a rube or anything like that. Not at all. Far from it. Just young was all he was trying to say. A kid. They were all kids.

Ted himself had grown up in Philadelphia, in a neighborhood, well, not so nice as this, if I knew what he meant. He laughed and winked and pulled on his nose. But it was all the same, he said. Big city, little town. Didn't matter. Boys were boys.

"We all had our girlfriends, you know how that is, and our football jerseys, and then all of a sudden the bells were ringing and school was out and everybody was saying how you oughta just go on and marry this girl or that girl and get some job dumb enough to put your mind to sleep for good, and then sure enough the kids would start coming, and so you'd just be going on like that all your life there in that same ugly neighborhood or that same dinky town until it was all over, and you were dead.''

That was why he had joined up anyway, he said, and most likely Gunar, too, from what he understood him to be saying about it. To break right out of that rut altogether before it got deep enough to drag you down and hold you in forever.

Of course, the reality of it was that boot camp came as a big surprise. It wasn't any football game, that was one thing sure. But those boys were tough enough, they could handle it all right. They could handle anything, just about. They went on and did whatever it was they were supposed to do. Nobody was thinking too much about Vietnam then. They knew that maybe that was where it all was leading up to, but that was okay, too, because they'd be ready for it and they were learning plenty of things they were getting real eager to start putting into practice.

Nobody knew politics from a hole in the ground.

Ted stretched out his long legs and rubbed his knees.

"The politics were all going on back here, I guess. Hell," he said, "even my own stupid little sister had enough nerve to come right out and tell me, right up to my face, after I got home, that I was some kind of goddamned baby killer. Why, I swear, I never killed no babies!"

He grinned again and flicked his tongue out between his teeth.

So, anyway, there they were, all of those boys in Vietnam, well aware now of just what it was they were up against. And their squad leader got killed somehow. Ted said he was one dumb bunny. He tipped back his head and sucked in a long whistle of air.

"They got him right here, laid him out real good."

He pointed to his chest and giggled behind his other hand.

"Fragged him."

Anyway, when that guy checked out like that, then Gunar was next in line to take over the squad, and everybody was more than satisfied with that arrangement, because, well, they liked the Dodge, is what.

"The Dodger, he was slick, oh, he was one slick puppy, that one," Ted said. "I guess you musta known that already." He could smell Charlie, it seemed like. Just always knew where he was. He took care of his squad, good care of them. At first, anyway.

"You know, it really killed him . . ." Ted Neeley coughed and blushed and worried a loose button on his shirt cuff. What he meant to say was how it tore Gunar up when he had to leave his men and come back here to Wizen River that one fall, the one before . . . the last time he was home. He didn't think he could ever trust anybody else to take care of those boys, his boys, he said, like he knew he was always going to be able to do.

But then the Dodger came back to Nam and to his position of squad leader, and maybe it was just his being away in the world for a while like that, but what happened when Dodge got back was he started acting flaky and making some pretty bad mistakes.

"I don't know what it was, really I don't, Mrs. Dietter-mann. See, I was off then on a little R and R, and when I left, well, even then, Dodger, he was acting pretty weird. He had this look he'd get, all glazed over like a guy that's blind, or when a dog flips up, you know, that ugly inside eyelid they've got, and sometimes, the Dodge, he'd go on looking like that for hours on end before he'd ever be able to snap out of it. So, anyway, they go out on this patrol, see, no big deal, routine stuff, except, well, it was an ambush is what it was. That Charlie's one sneaky little yellow bastard, anybody who's seen him'll come out and testify to that. And Dodger, well, maybe he was lost or something, who knows? I don't know. Sometimes it occurs to me that maybe he had finally just had it. Up to here, you know? Dinky dau.''

Ted was sitting up now, leaning forward with his elbows on his knees, fussing with that loose button so that I thought he was going to snap it right off, and wagging his head at me all the time he talked.

"He musta been lost, is all I can figure, Mrs. Diettermann," Ted said. "Just had to be. Because, see, what he did was to call in the eighty-ones, which is just what he shoulda done under the circumstances, except one thing. One very big thing. A small detail, a big thing. He called them in right down smack on top of himself. Who would do that? If it wasn't a mistake?" He looked at me, as if he thought I could give him an answer. "Wasted the entire squad, Mrs. Diettermann. Your son . . ." He shook his head and rubbed his palms together. "So, well, I guess you can see. I suppose you'd agree. He had to be lost. Musta been. What else? Musta had his grids all mixed up and turned clear around backwards or something. That had to be it. Couldn't have happened any other way."

Ted's head stopped its wagging, and his voice trailed off until it was all still and quiet in the house. I could hear the buzz of the refrigerator way back down the hall and in the kitchen.

Upstairs, in his bed, Bo was sound asleep.

Ted looked at me, and he grinned. "But, hey, Mrs. Diettermann," he said, "see, Gunar and me, we were friends, that's all. You gotta know that. Why, he told me just about everything there was to tell about this place and the people here. I know so much about it all, well, it's kinda like I grew up here myself, and, well, I guess I just had to come back here and see the whole thing for myself. You know, the park and the river and all of that."

He stood up then. He was very tall. He reached back into his pocket and pulled out a bulging black billfold. He stuck his finger and his thumb and daintily removed a small snapshot. He looked at it tenderly and then smiled and waved it in my direction.

"Neva Jolene Boots," he said solemnly. "See, he told

me all about her, too. He made her sound real good, if you know what I mean. Number one. Like she was a good person. Dodger, well, he talked about you and your gardens and this place and all, but when he got onto the subject of Neva Jolene, well, sometimes you just couldn't get him to shut his trap and stop. Wasn't her mama your cleaning lady or something? Yeah? See, I told you, the Dodge, he didn't hold back. A nice girl, a real good person, you know. He was real sweet on her, I don't know if you were aware . . . And then when he started to go all flaky like that, well, it was almost like he knew what was gonna happen next, 'cause, see, he gave me this picture. Of her. To keep.''

Ted brought the photo up close to his face, so close that his pupils practically disappeared crossing into one another, and then he kissed it one time with his wide, wet lips, slobbering all over it. "And I've been holding on to it, close to my heart, you might say, ever since." Then he handed it over to me.

It was an old photo, damp from what must have been many such affectionate smacks, and softened, as though it had been handled many times, and small, so I had to hold it up close, too, to really see it.

When I realized whose face it was, I gasped.

Ted was going on about how he just thought that with Gunar dead and all, well, he just thought maybe he'd come out her and get to know this girl, because he felt like he knew her so well already. If I knew what he meant, that was.

But the face in the photo that Lance Corporal Ted Neeley had waved and kissed and handed over to me didn't belong to Neva Jolene Boots. Those big blue eyes weren't hers. Nobody in that family had such long, dark hair. And there wasn't any big, ugly port-wine birthmark there, either.

This was Lacey. Lacey Tooker.

I said so to Ted. I told him that the girl in the picture that he had been carrying around and kissing and showing off to his friends all this time was not Neva Jolene Boots, but another girl whose name was Lacey Tooker, and who

156

wasn't even living in Wizen River anymore, but now she was out in California with her baby boy, whose father just happened to be that Casey Boots, Neva Jolene's brother. At first Ted didn't believe me. He sat back down hard on the sofa and seemed to just shrink right up inside of himself. He bit on his lip and closed his eyes tight. I was afraid that maybe he was going to start to blubber and cry.

"But Neva Jolene is here," I told him. And it had been Neva Jolene that Gunar was talking about, not Lacey Tooker, even if he couldn't quite bring himself to showing that face around. She was right downtown, working at Casey's if he ever wanted to see her, which I thought that he probably should, having come all this way already.

"Is she pretty?" he asked, looking at the photograph again, turning it over in his huge hands.

I told him he would have to judge that for himself.

He followed my advice and my directions, and he went to Casey's and kept his distance until he had gotten used to that other, less fair face. And then Neva Jolene, who thought that he was only being strange and shy, made the first move, and, next thing anybody knew, they had gone off and got married. But Neva Jolene had trouble staying faithful to Ted, or any man, and she went out on him, and when she did that and then threatened to move back home to her mother besides, Ted Neeley was so distraught that he tried to kill himself with a carving knife.

What was it about that face that kept making the boys want to die?

12

And Now Neva Jolene

DE MORTUIS NIL NISI BONUM

Casey's is right downtown, packed in snug between the bakery and the hardware store across the street from Center Park. It has a wide glass window out front with CASEY'S painted in black and gold glittering letters that arch up from one corner and then down again to the other, and a slim marquee on a pole above the door whose cryptic messages— A 2 GO WRHS; HAPY OUR 5-2-7; WELCOM BAK U; O SORY NJB—change from week to week and are only sometimes decipherable even to those who happen to be in the know.

It is the young people in Wizen River who patronize Casey's. They go in there to eat after a football game, to share a soda pop, to play with the pinball machines and the video games, to listen to their rock and roll, to dance and hold each other close.

Originally the building had housed the bookstore where Mona picked up the Latin primers that we so diligently pored over together on our Sunday afternoons. Its decrepit owner, a real crosspatch of a man, who had to be flattered and cajoled into parting with even the smallest and most trivial of his volumes, and who had seemed to me to be on his last legs even back when I was a little girl growing up, had refused to turn with the commercial tide and was driven out of business by the more modern and amiable link of a chain store in the mall that wasn't afraid to mix in lurid paperbacks and best sellers, magazines and calendars, and even comic books, too, with its regular stock of classic and modern literature.

The old man, who had hardly had a paying customer for going on almost five years straight then, finally fell off his ladder and died. He wasn't even missed until several days later when we noticed that he hadn't shown up for his regular appointment with the Doctor—one that he had kept faithfully since any of us could remember; he had suffered for many years from gout and a bad heart—and when we finally had looked everywhere and asked everyone whether they had seen him around or heard where he had gone off to, there was nothing for it but to break the lock on the shop door and take a peek inside.

They found his body all right, crumpled up and moldering there on the carpet beside the bottom rung of the ladder. The Doctor said then if it wasn't the fall itself that had killed him, then his heart had stopped when he saw he was on his way down. And since he seemed to have outlived by many years all his known relations, in spite of his temper and his heart, and long ago broken off any ties that might have bound him to anyone who might have been considered a friend, we took it on ourselves to see to it that he was properly laid to rest. And then we just locked the shop back up again, leaving everything there inside, just as it was and just as it had been for years and years already.

I suppose that none of us felt that it would be right to go thumbing through all his precious books. He wouldn't have liked it. Maybe someone who was just as scholarly and just as devoted as he had been would come along and take it all over. Phoebe said we ought to at least confiscate the furniture—there was one fine old table that she particularly had her eye on for her own living room—and Rob Murdock said it was a firetrap, but it all stayed right where it was anyway.

So then, finally, it wasn't a scholar at all who came along, but a young grease monkey, not anyone who was even interested in the books or the furniture, much less knowledgeable about them, but Casey Boots, who, together with his sister and his mother, had figured out that the old abandoned shop would be a good and profitable spot for opening up a place catering to the special thirsts and hungers of the Wizen River youth. And since no one else, besides Phoebe Tooker and her limited interest in a table, had shown even the smallest bit of desire for the place, the Boots family was able to buy it for themselves.

What Casey did was to leave all those books, and there were hundreds and hundreds of dim and dusty volumes stacked up from floor to ceiling on shelves that covered three of the four walls. He left the ladder, too, a heavy old oak thing that was hung by brass hooks from a rail that ran clear around the room up near the high ceiling. The fireplace stayed where it was, and the old furniture, too. Casey brought in some of his own tables—big wire spools that had been lacquered and lacquered, layer upon layer, until there was a thick coat of cloudy resin covering up the splinters and filling in the cracks—and camp chairs for the comfort of his customers. He built a long counter along one wall, put in a grill and a refrigerator, and fixed up two toilets out back.

It was Neva Jolene who had the business sense. She knew just how much they could charge for a hamburger and a shake. She dealt with the salesmen who came in, and she had a way with them that worked heavily on the side of the business. Although, with that charmingly shy smile of his and those soft blue eyes, Casey was better when it came to working face to face with the customers, it was Neva Jolene who turned Casey's into the kind of place that kept the kids coming back and laying down their quarters after school night after night.

In summertime Casey's was a dark and cool retreat from

160

the sizzling heat outside, and in winter it was cozy and warm with the fireplace and easy chairs and the hot cocoa that they served all day, and long into the frozen night. Neva Jolene came to me for the hanging plants. She put up the marquee out front and painted the black and gold glitter in the window. She suspended from hooks in the ceiling lanterns that flickered like candles and lent a mysterious and intimate look to the place and made it that much more appealing to all those young and romantic kids.

Neva Jolene, who had grown into a long-legged scarecrow of a woman as pale and bony as her mother had ever been, liked to take one of the comfortable upholstered chairs by the fireplace and sit there, a part of, and yet still very much keeping her distance from, the merrier crowd that swarmed around the tables. She would put herself in profile when she could, the bad side of her face hidden in the shadows. Some nights she might even climb up the ladder, and she might perch up there near the top of the shelves, where the books were dimmer and dustier than ever, for hours on end, overseeing all her customers as if they were really a small and inferior people over whom she could rule like some kind of a queen.

At first, in the beginning, she had worked alongside her brother, waiting on the tables and counting out the change. But when their clientele had swelled to include all those kids from other towns, too—some even came from as far off as Lincoln, brought there by rumor and word of mouth—and the money started practically rolling in, then Casey hired someone else to work the grill, and Neva Jolene took on a small fleet of younger, prettier girls who, in their awe of her, let her boss them around mercilessly.

Most nights, when Neva Jolene was maybe feeling just a little bit bored or restless, she might latch on to some farm boy who had come in looking for a willing girl to take for a ride in his pickup truck, and if he had the right look and the right lines, she would agree to go off with him.

Sometimes she would disappear for several days, and other times she was back in an hour.

Tongues had long since stopped their wagging over Neva Jolene Boots's escapades in Wizen River, and Casey had never been interested in keeping any kind of tabs on his sister's whereabouts. Even Mrs. Boots had given up trying to keep track. Like a cat, Neva Jolene came and went of her own free will. When it came to men, she was way beyond anybody's reach. She just liked them, that was all, and she had a way with them, too, that made them like her right back.

Neva Jolene Boots wasn't any real beauty, that was for sure. She was too tall and too gawky, and she had brown hair that was thick and dull and grew out like a brown, fuzzy cloud around her head. And then there was that blotch, the port-wine stain spreading out across her cheek. Sometimes it looked to me like some foreign continent; once I thought I could see in it the outline of a bear.

So maybe it was the stain itself, the blight that men with more stomach for that sort of thing than Casey—who preferred a clear, high-cheeked face like Lacey's—found appealing. Maybe her imperfection brought out something flawless in their souls that made them love themselves and her too, on the way. She told me once about how Gunar had touched it, how he said it changed color and darkened almost to purple whenever she laughed hard or got excited about something. Anger could turn it black, he said.

Whatever it was about Neva Jolene, though, it was true that she never did have any trouble finding herself some young man to come in and take her away from it all, if only for a short while. But none of them, not even Gunar Diettermann himself, had ever managed to keep her as his own for very long.

She was married only that one time, to Ted Neeley. Ted came into Casey's every night for a whole month just to sit there on one of the camp chairs and ogle Neva Jolene Boots. Maybe it took him that long to get used to the sight of her face. She really did become something special to that boy.

And, of course, she couldn't have missed all the attention he was paying her. She had a quick enough eye for that kind of thing. Finally, she figured out that if Ted was ever going to get brave enough to stop all his moony staring and get on with whatever business it was that he had reeling in his mind, she was just going to have to be the one to start it up. She came to him on a noisy, crowded Friday night; she held his hand, sat on his lap, wrapped her arms around his neck. Two weeks later, they had gone off and got married, and Neva Jolene had moved out of her mother's house and into a trailer outside town with her new husband.

Ted worshiped his bride. Probably she didn't know one thing about the picture of Lacey Tooker he had been carrying around thinking it was her for all that time after Gunar died. Sometimes he would be helping her up into the truck or holding her hand in his while they strolled around, looking in at the shop windows downtown.

"He's not like Gunar, Annie D.," she said to me. "Not one bit. But anyway . . . there's something . . . I can't quite tell you why."

She seemed just happy enough to let herself shine in the light of all his adoration, until after a while it must have worn her down, because she got caught slipping out Casey's back door under the tattooed arm of some man from the slaughterhouse.

Ted Neeley knocked the man down and sat on him and boxed his ears and broke his nose, and then he dragged Neva Jolene out to his truck and drove her home to their trailer. When they got there she started packing up her things and he stomped off into the tiny kitchen, took a carving knife down off its rack above the stove, and said to Neva Jolene Boots, "Watch this!" And then he drove the blade straight down into his own belly. They took him to the hospital in Omaha, and when he recovered, he was gone, just as quick as he had come. Neva Jolene moved back into the peach-colored house with Casey and Mrs. Boots.

"He was clearly demented," she said to me, shaking her wild hair and laying a palm up against the stained side of her face. "I guess I'm just not the marrying kind," she said, and shrugged.

Although I know she would have married Gunar, if she could.

It wasn't very long after Ted Neeley had so dramatically demonstrated to Neva Jolene just how deep his devotion to her was that she started to show up uninvited and unexpected at my house. Sometimes she came to trade in the old plants from the bar for some new ones. There was so little sunlight that managed to make its way into Casey's that we had to rotate the plants, bringing in new healthy ones when the old had begun to sicken and die, and taking the old ones out for me to nurse back to health again. Sometimes she only dropped in to say hello and to see how I was doing and to say hi to Bo. He liked to have her sit with him, hold his hand, play the radio, or read stories from the books that she found on the shelves in the café.

He got so her visits were making a difference to him, and he started looking forward to them. If she was gone for a while, he would worry until she showed up again. And then it got to be that Neva Jolene really began to make herself right at home in my house. It infuriated Phoebe to see her there, but I really didn't mind it all that much. I guess maybe I always just felt so sorry for her that turning her away seemed a harder thing to do than letting her come around.

Besides, she was good for Bo. Anybody with eyes could have seen the truth of that.

Sometimes I might come home from my shopping and there would be Neva Jolene in the living room leafing through the catalogues. "Here's a pretty little thing here, Annie D.," she would say, holding up the page for me to see. "Wouldn't you just love to have one of those for yourself?"

Or I might go outside in the late morning to do some weeding or replanting and find Neva Jolene stretched out there on the bench, sunning herself.

"Your garden is so pretty, Annie D.," she would say, her eyes hidden behind the mirrored glare of her sunglasses. "Truly a haven."

Or I would come downstairs for breakfast and there she would be, tousled and yawning, just waking up herself, on my sofa.

She was like a stray cat that just came and then went away again, and there was no telling when she might show up next.

Lacey and John Tooker's stay in Wizen River had stretched from a few days into a few weeks. Spring had stormed into summer, full of thunder and lightning and high winds and rain. My garden was deep and green and in wild bloom. The heat had settled down like a heavy, damp rag all around. John said that sometimes it made the air so thick he felt like he was walking through Jell-O, the way it rippled and rolled in the distance.

The kids had all come back out to mill around in the park again after dark. Two women were dead—one just a high school girl and the other a young mother—and their killer hadn't been caught, but people have short memories for pain, and they didn't really believe that their lives might be in jeopardy, especially the kids, who never seem to be able to accept the fact that it is possible for them to die. Some of them had parents who didn't care, who were just as happy to have their children out of the house. Others had to lie and sneak around, complaining that their mothers were over-protective, or that their fathers just didn't understand. The parents set up Neighborhood Watch committees, keeping a lookout for suspicious people or unfamiliar cars. Men bought guns and kept them loaded in their bedside table drawers. The hardware store sold out of slide bolts and padlocks. Families stewed in their beds at night, suffocating in the heat with their windows pulled shut and locked tight.

Rob Murdock put in extra hours and stepped up security in town, hiring on two new deputies to patrol Center Park on foot and instructing them to bring in anyone who looked out of the ordinary. They arrested an old bum who was found sleeping under a bench; Eddie Fly, who had been caught trying to steal a girl's purse; and some boys who were too young to be drinking beer out in the woods behind the Episcopal church.

Nancy Peters's husband had packed up his baby and taken a job in Florida where his mother lived. Tom Brady could still be seen drunk on the streets, going on and on about the end of the world and the Rapture, Armageddon and the Days of Darkness, floods and earthquakes and murder and disease, and some people had even started to listen to what he had to say. There was talk about how computers were the devil's work and the coded price lines on packages in the grocery store could bring evil and wickedness into innocent souls and steal them away. A group of Baptists tried to burn some rock and roll records, complaining that they were really satanic messages meant to corrupt the children who listened to them. One person even put forth, in a letter to the editor that was published on the second page of the *Gazette*, the theory that maybe a UFO had landed and aliens had abducted the women and used them for testing and then dumped them when they were done. That, the letter writer said, explained the missing hair sample and the way that the bodies had been left so neatly.

In truth, everyone was hoping that the problem would somehow go away. We were thinking, the way people do, that these bad things couldn't affect us, not really. Murder happened to other people, in other places. If Lynette Brady was dead, well, in some way she must have deserved it, or asked for it. People looked at her family and made judgments based on what they saw. The father is a drunk, they said. A fanatic. It was a shame, but the girl was unlucky, singled out, chosen for tragedy.

Jimmy Cline had quit the basketball team and could be seen hanging around the park, loitering, dressed all in black—jeans and torn T-shirts and boots—smoking cigarettes and keeping his thoughts to himself.

The *Gazette* was reporting, in increasingly brief articles, buried deeper and deeper among the ads in its back pages, that Rob Murdock was maintaining a strict silence on any leads that he might have about who the killer may have been, but everyone assumed that that was only his way of not admitting to the truth, which was that he had no idea.

Lacey Tooker, after a lot of embarrassed and apologetic beating around the bush, asked me one night if I would baby-sit with John while she went down to Casey's. Not that John was a baby or anything like that, she said. He was almost nine years old, after all, and she had left him alone plenty of times back home, but only after school and never at night, and that was an apartment building, with lots of neighbors close by, within shouting distance, some of them, but her mother's house, well, it was just so all alone up there on the hill with the woods on every side even if it was only Wizen River, and then there were those two poor dead women to think about, too. Well, she just wouldn't feel right about leaving him. Not that she absolutely had to go out or anything. She didn't have to, of course, and if there was a problem, well, she just wouldn't, that was all. Or she could take him with her, she guessed. It was only that Casey had asked her, and he was being so nice about everything, and so she was thinking that she just might take him up on it and go, but if it would mean any bother for me, if I really did mind having to watch him for her, she could stay home.

She paused, breathless, her eyes glittering.

I made it easy for her and said I would be happy to help out. I liked John Tooker; he was a nice, polite boy.

Since Lacey had come back home to Wizen River, Bo had been spending more of his time out on his own, alone or with his old friends, because I just couldn't keep on watching him all the time like that, even if I was his mother and had a right to be always worrying about him. But he hadn't been feeling well at all that day. I heard him talking to himself in his room when I stopped to listen outside the door.

He did that sometimes. Lots of people do. I do it myself

now and then. I talk to my flowers. It's because I get lonely, I guess. And Bo was lonely, too. He had closed so many doors inside himself. He was living in some empty, hollowed-out rooms.

He had come downstairs once, later that afternoon, but by the time his foot hit the bottom step, he had forgotten what it was he was after, and he turned around and plodded back up the stairs and into his room again, closing the door behind him.

It was just the heat, he said, when I peeked in to check that he was all right.

It gave him headaches, like some giant had stepped inside his head, squeezing on his brain. Like elephants in the dark. Like salamanders squirming on the floor.

It made his sight foggy and his eyes glazed. His bare feet were slick with sweat. He stayed in his room, where it was quiet and cool, with the fan blowing a breeze down on him from above the bed, and he didn't come downstairs again even when Lacey and John Tooker arrived.

John was already in his pajamas, thin-striped ones that hung too baggy and short so his legs and slippered feet looked narrow and frail. He had had his supper already, and his bath, too. His hair was still damp and slicked back off his face. He was carrying a plastic sack of crayons and markers and a small pad of drawing paper under one arm; his other hand gripped his mother's. She nudged him gently forward with her knees, through the doorway and into the hall.

"He'll go to bed soon," Lacey said. "He's brought his colors." She smiled at me. She was still, in her way, apologizing for the imposition; still afraid that maybe she had overstepped some invisible bounds by asking me to do her this favor. She was used, after all these years, to taking care of things by herself. She didn't like to have to ask. She didn't want to have to need.

Then she turned and stooped to be at eye level with her son. She was wearing her hair loose that night, and it was so long that it touched the floor by his feet when she knelt beside him, and I guess it was ticklish on his skin, because he laughed.

"Be good, John, okay? No trouble for Annie D.? She's a nice lady, right? Have fun. She knows about little boys. She likes them a lot." Lacey looked up at me and smiled.

John nodded and patted Lacey's hair and gazed into her eyes so long and hard that I began to wonder what it was he was looking for there, but finally he took his hand away and smiled, and she kissed him and stood back up straight on her feet.

"He really will fall asleep soon," she said. "Anywhere almost. He's pretty tired. On the floor or the sofa—don't put yourself out, please. Whatever works best for you."

I had already made up Gunar's old bed for John.

"And," Lacey went on, "don't feel you have to wait up or anything like that. I'll just sneak in to get him, if that's okay."

I told her that yes, that would be just fine. I wouldn't wait up. She knew where I kept the spare key tucked into the dirt under the third brick back from the step in the front walk.

She kissed John again and ran her fingers through his hair, mussing it. Then the door slipped shut behind her, and she was gone.

John stood with his thin, small back to me, his head cocked slightly to one side, staring at the door, listening to the clip-clap of Lacey's sandals down the walk, the creak of the front gate, the thump of the car door as it shut, the revving up of the engine. Not until the sound of the motor had faded off on its way downtown did John turn back to me.

"She's gone," he said simply. He looked around, craning a little to see past me to the rest of the downstairs, as if he were trying to find the place where he would plant himself for the evening.

"You can sleep in Gunar's bed," I said. I took his small, clean hand and led him up the stairs.

He walked around Gunar's room, examining all his things. Gunar's medals were mounted on velvet in a black metal frame. A jar of coins sat on the desk. John looked at it and touched his fingertip to the glass.

"Coins," he said.

"My son collected them," I told him.

He beamed. "Me too!" he said, as if that was a coincidence too far-fetched to be believed. "I collect them, too. I have pesos from Mexico, and francs. All kinds of stuff. My mom gets them for me." He looked at me.

"I have some German coins in the attic," I said. "You could have them, if you want."

"German?"

"Deutsche marks," I said. "My husband was from Germany. He grew up there. Before the war."

I was thinking that John would like to come back down to the living room with me until it was time for bed. I had baked cookies that afternoon, and I had pulled out some of the boys' old games for us to look at and maybe play.

But he said, "I'll just stay here, I think. If that's okay."

He seemed pleased to note that Gunar's window faced out front to the street, where he could see his mother come back to get him. And he wasn't hungry, thank you, he'd already brushed his teeth anyway, but he would like a glass of water, please, and then he would get into bed and do his drawing there, if that was all right with me.

"I won't get any colors on the sheet, Annie D. I never do. I promise," he said.

He smiled so his teeth showed, small and white and sharp, and climbed up into bed, and after he had pushed back the blanket, because it was too hot to want to be covered up by anything much at all, he asked if I would please leave his door open for his mother. So she would be able to find him all right.

"But you don't really want to go to bed now, do you?" I asked. "It's early yet."

I have to admit that I was annoyed. I had been looking forward to spending a little time with him alone.

"Oh, yes, I do," he said. "I've had a long day." He smiled and looked at me, waiting for me to go away.

When I came back downstairs, after hovering about in the hall, waiting for John to change his mind and join me after all and wondering whether I should disturb Bo, just in case he needed anything, there was Neva Jolene in the chair by the front window, with her legs tucked up under her, leafing through a magazine, listening to the TV. She took me by surprise. I hadn't heard her come in, and the sudden sight of her gave me a fright.

"Hello," she said, grinning at me so that her birthmark scrunched up into the creases around her mouth. "I let myself in." She held up the key to my front door, dangling it between her forefinger and thumb so that it glittered in the lamplight. "You shouldn't leave this out there, Annie D. Anybody could find it, you know. Everyone knows where you hide it, and anyone at all could use it to come in."

I took it from her and put it into my pocket, thinking I would just wait up for Lacey, and unlock the door for her myself.

Neva Jolene told me that she had left Casey's because it was so quiet and so strange in there these days, what with the murders and all.

The darkness of the night outside seemed to be pressing up against my windows. I checked the locks and pulled the curtains shut.

"And anyway," Neva Jolene went on, "I was worried about you, Annie D." All alone, defenseless and on my own, in this house and everything.

But I think she really only came by in order to avoid meeting up with Lacey and maybe to see John, too. He was her nephew, after all.

"John's in bed," I said.

She swung her legs around onto the floor and stood up. "Good," she said, setting the magazine back down on the coffee table again. "I'll just go up and tuck him in, then."

"I did that."

"I'll do it again."

I thought that it was just as well she wasn't hanging around Casey's that night. It didn't seem right for anybody

171

to be going off with strangers that summer, not when one of them could have been a rapist and a killer with a hair collection and more in mind than a few hours out under the stars in the back of a truck with a girl like Neva Jolene Boots.

But there wasn't any telling, either, what kind of an awkward thing she might come up with to say to John.

I followed her upstairs and listened from the hall, just outside the door.

John was propped up against the pillows, drawing on a pad of blank paper.

"Whatcha making?" Neva Jolene asked, sitting down on the edge of the bed, rocking it so that John's crayon wobbled on the page.

He didn't look at her. "Nothing," he said.

"Well, it's gotta be something if you're drawing it," said Neva Jolene. She craned to see, but he tipped it up and away, out of her view.

"Okay," he said, "then it'll be you." He put one crayon back and carefully selected another.

"I'm your aunt, you know," she said.

"Yeah, I know."

"Your dad's my brother."

"I know that."

"We're related, you and me."

Neva Jolene got up and went over to the window. She stood there, looking out, until John put down his crayons and held out the picture he had been drawing for her to see.

"It's you," he said again. He folded his arms across his chest and watched her looking at the picture.

"That's real nice, John," said Neva Jolene. She bent over and kissed him on the forehead. "Thank you," she whispered. "Go to sleep."

He rolled over onto his side, and Neva stood looking at him for a minute before she turned away. I hurried down the hall and down the stairs and was in the kitchen getting cookies and tea when Neva Jolene finally came in. She laid the picture on the table and went back to looking at her magazine in the chair by the window.

I picked up my knitting.

The picture that John had colored was of a face, with a halo of brown hair billowing out around it. Wide blue eyes looking calmly out. A round nose. A smiling mouth. And his rendering of the birthmark—half the face was patterned in an elaborate, beautiful, many-colored design, as intricate and lovely as the marks on a butterfly's wing.

"It's me," said Neva Jolene, touching her face with the tip of her finger.

"I could tell."

Neva Jolene stayed tucked up where she was and read her magazine and watched TV, nibbling on cookies and sipping at her tea, while my hands worked and my needles clicked. Sometimes she would sigh and fan herself and comment about how it sure was hot, and I would nod and knit and agree that yes, it was hot.

Then at last we heard the car pull up and saw the lights blink off, and Neva Jolene peeked through the curtains to watch Lacey come up the walk. Lacey tapped timidly at the door and seemed a little surprised when I opened it. She hadn't expected me to still be awake. She thought that everyone would be in bed.

"I told you not to wait up," she said. "The key's not there . . ." She didn't see that Neva Jolene was with me until I led her into the living room. "Oh, hi." She smiled stiffly at Casey's sister.

Neva Jolene grinned back. "Hi, Lacey. Long time no see."

Lacey sat down on the edge of the sofa, across from Neva Jolene. She picked up John's drawing off the table and looked at it.

"He said that it's a portrait of me," Neva Jolene told her. "Nice kid."

Lacey raised her eyebrows. "Thanks," she said. "I was at Casey's. Nice place."

"Thanks."

The two women looked at each other. Lacey cleared her throat and pushed her hair back behind her ear. "I like the hanging plants. And the books. They make the place, well, cozy, I guess. Homey. Give it character, you know . . ."

"Pretty empty tonight, huh?" Neva Jolene asked.

That strangler business. That was why.

Lacey shivered and shook her head. "I had sort of a close call myself once . . ." she began. That was when she told us about the man who had broken into her apartment in California on the same night she got the telegram from me saying that her mother was dead. The locks on the door; the shadow in the drapes; the pantomime in the manager's window; John falling off his bike into the grass; the razors and ropes that they found laid out on the bed in her room.

"That's why I came back here, I guess," Lacey said. "And, of course, because of my mother, too."

"You can't be too careful, honey," I said.

Lacey laughed nervously. "I thought we'd at least be safe here," she said. "In Wizen River, I mean. Nothing used to ever happen here, did it?"

Neva Jolene laughed. "I guess not," she said. "Not much anyway."

Lacey stood up. "Where's John?" she asked.

I told her he was up sleeping in Gunar's bed.

"You could leave him here," I said. "He could just spend the night."

Neva Jolene fingered her birthmark and watched Lacey. Lacey stretched out her hand, and her long, painted nails glistened. She buffed them against the side of her leg.

"Well, no," she said, stretching. "Thank you, Annie D., but I really couldn't impose. I should be going. It's late. Annie D., thank you, but I guess maybe I ought to just take him home. That's what I told him I would do. It's what he's expecting. He doesn't much like surprises." She looked at Neva Jolene again. "Kids never do," she said.

When we went upstairs we found that John wasn't

sleeping in the bed after all, but had curled up with his pillow on the floor under the window. He must have tried to wait up and watch for his mother to come home. His crayons and paper were on the bed.

"He loves to draw," Lacey said, carrying him out. He looked so big and awkward and heavy, with his head lolling back against her shoulder and his feet dangling off her arm.

Lacey went home, and I went to bed. I left Neva Jolene Boots still watching TV in the chair by the window, with a beer hanging off one hand and her feet up on the table, crossed.

And John's beautiful picture of her looking back.

I heard Bo clatter out early the next morning, on his way to work cleaning up the trash in the park. His headache must be better, I thought. I was glad of it, too. I was just making a pot of coffee for myself when Lacey phoned to thank me one more time for minding John. I told her I was happy to help and she should feel free to call me any time.

What we didn't know, but found out soon enough, was that Neva Jolene was walking home in the middle of the night after Lacey left, and she had been attacked by whoever it was that had killed those other two girls.

They found her body under the bleachers by the baseball diamond out back behind the school, and she had been raped, all right, and she had been strangled, too, and she was missing a big chunk of her dull, cloudy brown hair.

"Probably that Ted Neeley. Sounds exactly like some crazy thing he would do. Doesn't it? Doesn't it?"

That was what Bo, thoughtfully chewing on his toast and spewing out a fine spray of crumbs as he spoke, said to me on the morning after we had laid poor Neva Jolene Boots's body to rest. Mrs. Boots had been hysterical. She was in a lot of pain besides because of her arthritis. Her hands, when she brought them up to cover her mouth and stop the croaks and groans that kept leaking and popping out, were all humped up and knotted at the knuckles, just like the tangled, twisted roots of an old, dead tree. Casey stood on one side of her, and Lacey on the other.

Then Casey said it too, about Ted Neeley, and Rob Murdock started to look into where that boy might have gone. It was something to do, and it seemed to make sense.

And it was the only lead he had.

13

The Truth About Bo

When Rob Murdock took on the job as our chief of police in Wizen River, he never counted on having to deal with anything like the horrible crimes that were being committed over and over again that summer when Lacey and John Tooker came back to town after Phoebe's car climbed the oak tree on the hill up by the Tooker Place. All he'd had to deal with up until then had been some family squabbles, like when that poor woman's husband beat her up so badly that she lost the baby that had been at the bottom of the argument in the first place; petty theft, like what Eddie Fly kept on carrying out all over town after he gave up pumping gas and working on the cars to make ends meet; vandalism, like the time some kids sneaked out and spray-painted a big blue peace sign on the brick wall outside the school; car accidents, like Phoebe Tooker's spectacularly fatal one; and speeders, outside town on the gravel roads that cut straight between the fields from one farm to another.

Rob Murdock was a handsome, unambitious man. He swaggered around town with his gunbelt and his nightstick clanking heavily on his hips, his silver badge a shining sun on the pocket of his blue shirts. He was one of Jack Tooker's cronies back in the days when Jack got fed up with all of Phoebe's grousing around and filed for divorce. Rob had been the friend who was crazy enough to go out ice-fishing in the Wizen River with Jack Tooker that one frozen morning in March when everybody else had the sense to stay inside where it was warm, and so he was there when Jack slipped and fell in under the ice. He loved to tell about how Jack Tooker went down. Everybody with ears had heard the story more than once.

When Lynette Brady was found in the park, raped and strangled and shorn, Rob's first guess had been that it was her boyfriend Jimmy Cline who did it. Then, when Nancy Peters's body was found by those boys down under the bridge by the river, Rob said that maybe it was just some drifter who had been passing through town and with any luck would be moving on again soon, out of his jurisdiction anyway. But when Neva Jolene Boots was dead, too, Rob really did have to start getting serious about what had been going on and take into consideration that maybe our killer was someone all of us knew.

He called in the sheriff's department for help and started questioning everybody who might know anything at all about what had happened that night. That meant me, and it included Lacey Tooker, too. I don't think either one of us was much of any help.

Except I did tell him about Ted Neeley and how he had come to my house with Lacey Tooker's picture in his wallet, thinking her face belonged to Neva Jolene.

Up until that night when Neva Jolene was murdered in the ballfield, Casey Boots and Lacey Tooker had been keeping a lid on what was becoming rekindled between them. It seemed like neither one of them was really too anxious to go starting it all up again. They knew what trouble was.

I think that maybe Casey had been considering how there was John now and that fact by itself made it all that much more serious between him and Lacey. He could probably remember how it had been before when they were both young and free enough still to see their romance as if it were just an exciting adventure and not anything that might have any strings attached to it. Casey certainly hadn't jumped up and run off to California to be with Lacey back then when she must have really been needing him. Maybe he just didn't want to sour up any of the leftover sweetness that went with all those memories of his.

At first Lacey had been full of enthusiasm about how she thought she would have to sell the Tooker Place and what kind of a price she might be able to ask for it and how much less than that somebody might be able to pay for it— enough, she was hoping, that she could scrape together what it would take to put a down payment on a house of her own in California. But the house and the grounds were badly in need of at least superficial repair—Phoebe hadn't ever been very handy with anything much heavier than a needle and thread—and Lacey would have to see to all of that if she was going to be able to get anything near what she should for the place.

She began with the painting of the whole outside. Bo started doing it for her himself, and Lacey put up some fuss about that because he really wasn't looking well by then, but when he argued and insisted, it was too hard to say no.

She gave in and hired him, and he got started. The going was slow, because he wasn't always up to the work—and he was easily distracted, too, leaning off into one of his trances, fading away for minutes, caught by the texture of the paint and the color of the sky—but still, he did manage to get most of the job done, and very well, too, all things considered. The fresh paint made the gardens look so bad by comparison that Lacey had to go to work on them, clearing out the tangles of weeds and dead grass and laying out flowers and bushes in their place.

And there were all the things inside the house to be taken care of, besides. Photo albums and magazines and dishes and silver and old clothes and old shoes and furniture and rugs. Lacey had planned on holding an auction up there, but

179

the job of sorting through everything was such a huge one that she never even made a dent in all the things that had, over the past thirty-odd years, been accumulating in the attic and the basement and the closets and the cupboards and the drawers.

Lacey would tie up her long hair and roll up her sleeves and set to work putting some of it in order, only to get herself distracted by some trinket or toy that brought back so many memories, good ones and bad ones, too, as to make the job itself almost unbearable. Then she'd pull away and put the thing back where she'd found it, and close the door on it all.

By late July, Lacey and John had been in Wizen River for almost two months, and Neva Jolene was dead and buried, and Casey had been coming around more and more often and staying over longer and longer at the house up on the hill. As long as it was summertime, so John wasn't missing any school, then Lacey could go on living in limbo, not quite settled in Wizen River, but still making no plans for going back to California either.

What Lacey had been doing all that time was to get herself in deeper and deeper with Casey Boots until finally she moved out of her old bedroom and into the one that had been Jack and Phoebe's room across the hall. And then Casey moved himself in there with her, too. He started by staying over, night after night, and then it got to be easier just to bring his things in there than to always have to be going home to get dressed in the morning before he went to work. And because Mrs. Boots—except for when she could put her mind and her body to rest with the sleeping pills that the new doctor kept on prescribing for her—was always so achy and ill, what with Neva Jolene gone and the arthritis and all, Casey hated the idea of leaving her all alone any more than he had to. He brought her on up there to the Tooker Place, too, and she took the guest room down the hall in the back upstairs corner of the house.

Then John, who all his life had been without any relatives

except his mother, had a father and a grandmother besides.

Mrs. Boots, when she was awake, which wasn't often anymore, or for very long, said over and over how much John looked just like Casey had when he was a kid. She told me that there were times when she truly got confused and imagined time had somehow slipped and it was Casey standing there with his hands in his pockets when really it was only John. I remembered how Mrs. Boots's bony hand could swipe out and redden a young boy's cheek when there was any trouble, and I only hoped that John was as smart as he looked and would know enough to just steer clear.

Lacey had started to talk about how it might be fun to spend a whole long year in Nebraska and get to know again what weather was.

Rob Murdock hadn't been able to locate the whereabouts of Ted Neeley yet, but there were posters with his picture on them tacked up to the bulletin board inside the grocery store and being circulated through all the small towns around the state.

While he and his hobbled mother were moving in and establishing themselves as full-time residents up at the Tooker Place—heedless of the gossip on all the wagging tongues in Wizen River—and while Bo was still at work putting a fresh coat of white paint on the outside boards of the house, Casey Boots was doing his very best to close up all the years that had come between him and his son.

The fatherhood that Casey kept bringing to John was an awkward and inexperienced one. Casey had hardly had a father of his own, and so he really didn't have anyone to imitate. John responded to Casey's clumsiness as if it were a well-meant but inappropriate gift. He tolerated his father and tactfully corrected him, and maybe even felt a little sorry for him, too. Casey was trying so hard to have the closeness that he believed a father ought to have with his own son, and John did seem to appreciate the effort. Sort of.

Lacey phoned on Wednesday to invite me and Bo up to

the Tooker Place for dinner on Sunday afternoon. It was her way, she said, of saying thank you to me for watching John that one night when she went down to Casey's, when Neva Jolene was killed, and to Bo for the slow but steady progress that he'd been making with the paint.

Lacey did a very nice job with her roast. The house was almost as tidy and clean as Phoebe had ever kept it, and if the potatoes were a little sticky, at least the gravy was rich and thick, and we all enjoyed the meal and each other's company very much. We went outside and sat on the porch with coffee after dinner.

Bo was in his overalls, still splattered in places with dried paint, and he sat hunched up on the top step of the porch with his elbows on his knees. He grinned at Lacey whenever she looked his way. He was wearing his green baseball cap, and maybe he laughed too much, too often, too loud. The scars on the skin under his chin were thin, translucent almost, and white. Like worms.

John was sitting on the porch swing with his mother, and he had his dark head laid softly down in her lap. She poked her hand down under the collar of his shirt and scratched his back in gentle circles with her nails. He asked me again about the German coins that I had promised him, and I said I'd go up into the attic and bring them down first thing when I got home that night.

Then Casey came out into the yard with a football and called, "Come on, John, throw a few with me here."

John looked at his mother, and then at me, and, shrugging, pulled himself up to his feet. "Well, I'm probably not gonna be very good . . ." he said, shoving his hands down into his pockets.

"Aw, forget that," said Casey. "I'll teach ya . . ."

He stood in the middle of the lawn with the football held easily in the palm of one hand. "Okay, Johnny, run out that way, for a pass."

John looked at his father and then in the direction that he was pointing. "Couldn't you just throw it to me regular first?" he asked.

182

"Go on, run out there. Just try it. I'll throw it real gentle. I promise."

John pulled his hands out of his pockets, sighing, and looked back over his shoulder again. He shrugged and turned and began to run, the white soles of his sneakers flashing in the grass. He went out about ten yards and turned as Casey lobbed the ball. It spun in a pretty arc toward John, whose arms were outstretched to catch it, and it came down hard, bouncing wildly away. John dove for it and fell sprawling in the grass, the wind knocked out of him, gasping.

Lacey jumped to her feet.

Bo giggled into his hand.

Casey ran after the boy and knelt over him. And then he started poking at him, trying to rouse him up and maybe set him off giggling or something. But John was hurt and embarrassed, and he scowled and pushed Casey's hand away.

Casey wasn't one to know when to quit, and so he kept it up. Pretty soon the two of them were rolling around on the grass together, gasping and groaning as John fought to free himself from Casey's grasp. At last Casey let him go, and John, who was flushed and rumpled and close to tears, headed across the lawn toward the porch, where Lacey stood leaning on the railing, holding herself back from coming in between the two of them.

That was when Casey rushed him from behind and took John by surprise. He grabbed the boy and swung him up high in the air over his head.

John just wasn't one for that kind of rough-and-tumble. All that sweat and brawn was a torture to him. When his screams of protest brought no relief at all from Casey's affectionate but overpowering manhandling, John, as a last resort, let himself go limp all over, passive to any and all of Casey's maneuvers.

And that was what made Casey mad. He shoved the boy away and kicked out at him, only just missing as John rolled out of range. John scrambled straight on over to his mother and hid behind her legs. Bo, who had been rocking back and forth and clapping his hands, stifled a laugh. John's face was red and his ears were on fire and he wouldn't pull away, even when Lacey tried to push him back so she could look at his face and wipe away his tears.

Casey came up and stood before the two of them, his hands hanging at his sides. He sat down next to Lacey and put his arm around her, slow and gentle now.

"I'm sorry, John," he said, "I didn't mean to hurt you."

It was just that Casey loved the boy so much he couldn't keep his hands off.

Lacey reached out and touched Casey's cheek. She turned him toward her and pulled his face down close to hers.

"It's okay, Casey," she whispered, "we love you." She hoisted John up onto Casey's lap, and Casey held the boy on his knees and rubbed his shoulders with his free hand. John leaned back against his father's chest and, closing his eyes, he allowed himself to be nuzzled there.

When I looked at Bo, I could see that he had gone off again, staring, lost somewhere in the color and the texture of Lacey's beautiful hair.

The Doctor died of cancer in 1966, before Gunar became a soldier, when he and Bo were still only boys in their teens. The cancer affixed itself to the very marrow of his bones, and then it ate him up alive, from the inside.

We tried everything from herbs and vitamins to cortisone and chemotherapy to keep him from being consumed, until his skin crackled and his greasy black hair all fell out. But nothing worked. Nothing brought relief. The Doctor's body was invaded by a host of alien cells, parasites that grew and multiplied, at a measured and incessant rate, until he couldn't function anymore, not even in the simplest, most natural of ways. He shriveled and shrank in upon himself, just like the Wizen River in July.

And then there wasn't one thing I could do for him. Nothing but stand by faithfully with Darla Williams and

184

watch him writhe and groan in utter misery, seeing to it that at least his linens were fresh and his pillows plumped and trying to keep the boys busy and out of the house as much as I could just so they wouldn't have to share in the sights and sounds of their father's last gasps, until finally the Doctor was in the hospital, and then he was dead.

Then I had to find some place to put all the medical equipment that he had left behind in his examining room. I gave almost all of it, along with all the records of his patients, away to the new young doctor who had come to set up his own practice in Wizen River. I cleared out the room completely, boxing up the scalpels and clamps and other small tools that I kept, and, because it was such a bright, sunny place with all the windows facing so perfectly to the south and to the east, I brought in all my potted plants and how they did thrive in there and still do even now.

I stored the boxes up in the attic along with the two big steamer trunks that the Doctor had brought over with him when he first left Germany to come live here with us.

One trunk was filled with old pictures, and in the other hung old clothes. The pictures were of the Doctor's home and his family. Gunar and Jan and little Else in funny hats and clothes, posed in the shadows of Gothic cathedrals or against a background of clear, green, rolling hills. They were places that always looked just like paradise to me.

And in one of the drawers of one of the steamer trunks there were some coins, Deutsche marks, that I had promised to give to John Tooker Boots, which is what he had taken to calling himself by then.

What I did was this. I told John about the German coins and said that he could have them.

I had to go up into the attic to get them out of the drawer in the steamer trunk in the corner at the back. There weren't very many of them, and they probably weren't worth a thing.

Maybe I should have just left it alone.

Because, as I was turning to climb back down the stairs

with the coins cupped in the palm of my hand, a gleam of metal in the corner by the wall caught my eye.

I almost let it go. I almost didn't stop to take a look. But then my curiosity got the better of me, and when I was all the way down to the bottom of the stairs, and just about to step through the door into the hallway between the bedrooms again, well, I slipped the coins into the pocket of my apron, and I turned around, and I went back up.

It was so hot and so musty and so dirty there in that corner, that I almost changed my mind again and let it be. I wasn't so sure that I really wanted to go poking with my bare hand in those dark shadows with all the dust and the cobwebs and maybe even bugs or spiders, too. But then the light from the bare bulb overhead caught the glint of the metal again, and it winked up at me, and so I just sucked in my breath and crouched down low and closed my eyes and groped until my hand hit the cold, hard surface of a small steel box.

I pulled it out and turned it over and over in my hands. It was the kind of strongbox that some people use to lock up their most valuable papers and keep them safe from fire or theft. The lock was already battered and broken; the hinges were rusted and cracked. I couldn't guess what it was or where it had come from or who had put it there in the corner of the attic like that.

The thought did cross my mind that maybe I had found something of value, some treasure that had been sitting there all those years, forgotten, just waiting for the right moment, just hoping to be remembered and retrieved.

I sat there for a while on the floor of the attic, and I held that metal box in my lap, looking at it, feeling its weight heavy on my knees. I thought about not opening it up at all. I considered just putting it right back where I'd found it. That would have been a simple enough thing for me to do. It was so odd what a chill I was getting just to look at the thing.

But then I thought how foolish I was being over some old box, and so I did go ahead, and I did open it up.

The hinges squeaked and squealed as I lifted the lid. And I knew then what it was that had made me feel so afraid.

Inside that box, the one I had found in my own attic—just because that Lacey Tooker had come back and taken up with Casey Boots again, so I had John one night and he touched Gunar's jar on the table by the bed and told me he collected coins; and just because the man that I had married had happened to live in Germany when the Nazis came along, and he had lost his family and left his memories behind, and he had been a doctor, and Wizen River had needed a doctor, and my mother hadn't been satisfied with her life but had dreamed of things bigger and better than the cornfields and the pigsties, and so she had taught me Latin and thought that somehow that would help me teach him English, and because of what he had been and where he had come from he had been anxious to settle back down again, and so he had taken me for his bride, and I had borne him two sons, only to see one die in a terrible war and the other one . . . well . . . and the Doctor had died, too, and left all of his old things in two trunks and some cartons up there in my attic. And just because I had then gone and gotten the German coins. And just because the light had been so right that it happened to catch the glint of metal as I was climbing back down the stairs . . .

Just because . . .

Inside that box that I had pulled out from the shadows, even though there were cobwebs and dirt and maybe even bugs and spiders, too . . . Inside that box were three clear waxed-paper envelopes.

And inside each of those envelopes there was a clump of hair.

And inside the one envelope that I pulled out and held up to the light, the hair was dark and smoky, like a cloud.

I didn't look in either of the other two envelopes.

I knew whose hair it was that was tucked away into them. In one envelope it would be blond and silky; in the other it would be coarse and red.

I put the first envelope back into the box, and then I

187

closed the lid down again, and then I put the whole thing back in the corner where I had found it. And then I climbed down the stairs, and then I switched off the light, and then I pulled the door softly shut against the darkness behind me.

I should have said something, but I didn't. I never breathed a word of it. I couldn't tell a soul. I could guess what they would do to him. Lock him up. Take him away. Put him away. Hospitalize him, because it couldn't have been his fault. Institutionalize him. In small rooms, with long shadows, behind heavy bars.

Already there had been too much. Bo was my son. He was my child. It was my job . . . it was my duty . . . I was his mother, and mine would always be the burden of seeing to it that he was kept safe and away from harm.

I turned off the light, and I closed the door, and I went downstairs, and I got into bed, and I went to sleep, and I tried to forget.

14

The Truth About
Annie D.

CONFITEOR

It was the clomp and drag of Bo's work boots in the hall that roused me awake, out of my clogged dreams and back into the starker commonplace of Wizen River, Nebraska, again. I lay in bed and listened to him as he paused and scuffed at the landing, shifting the weight of his empty canvas trash bag over to the other shoulder, maybe, straightening his baseball cap so that it would rest just so, pulled down low on his brow. And then he tromped on down that last short flight into the hall. The front door squeaked open, banged shut.

Another one of our fierce summer mornings had dawned; already the flies and the mosquitoes and the bees and the gnats had begun their whiz and drone. A good, hard rain couldn't have broken through that thickening heat outside. It would have done no better than to leave the air more sodden and more ponderous than ever.

I scrambled up out of my bed and over to the window at the far side of the room. The floorboards seemed to steam. I leaned against that one chair that had been the Doctor's, the one that Neva Jolene Boots had sat in that spring morning after they came to tell me about how Gunar was dead in the war, and before Bo . . .

I peeked out through the glass at my son as he left the house. I was poking my little finger in through a ragged burnhole in the arm of the chair, and I could feel the softer stuffing underneath. I was thinking, again, that I would have to have that poor old chair reupholstered someday. Maybe in white this time—that would be pretty, and fresh.

Bo shuffled down the front walk. He was so thin that he looked like his bones would break. His baseball cap was the green color of the grass. Tufts of his dark hair poked out from underneath it in the back and lay softly there against the smooth pale skin of his nape. He had his bag slung back over one shoulder so that it bumped against his hip as he walked. He held his pick as though it were a flagstaff. The white pants that he wore were baggy and torn at the cuffs; one of the leather laces to his boots was untied and it straggled along dangerously between his feet.

I wanted to open the window and cry out after him. "Bo! Tie your shoe!"

He was on his way to work over at the park.

He reached out and unlatched the front gate at the end of the walk, and he turned back toward the house as he carefully closed it behind him, and when he turned like that, I could see that his mouth was moving, his lips were squirming. He must have been murmuring something to himself. Or maybe he was singing. When he looked up at my window, he didn't seem to see that I was there watching him, because he didn't wave, he turned away, and then he disappeared behind the hedge.

I dressed quickly, throwing on my clothes. I didn't stop even to brush my teeth or comb my snarly hair. I splashed water on my face. I rushed out of the house and down the street after my only boy.

The pavement was wavering in the heat.

Eddie Fly was there in the park, lounging on his bench near the duck pond. His short legs were stretched out as far as

190

they would go; he had his arms flung open wide and spread across the top rail of the bench; his head was tilted back so I could see his seamed and grizzled throat; he squinted into the sun, absorbing all that heat right down into his cold, old bones. It must have felt good. Sweat dripped down his temples to his chin and hovered there.

I could see Casey Boots across the street in front of his café, swiping a rag over the glass of the front window, making the arch of glittered letters sparkle and shine. There were two small children, a boy in a red cap and a girl with yellow pigtails, digging for treasure in the sand at the playground. Their mothers sat nearby on a blanket in the grass, sipping coffee out of white foam cups and smoking cigarettes and chatting quietly. In the panes of their mirrored sunglasses were the infinite reflections of their own faces, caught.

I glimpsed the quick flash of Bo's green cap through the trees at the far end of the playground. When I came closer, I could see that he was only doing his job, stabbing at the papers and the gum wrappers and the empty cups with his long, thin poker. He was whistling through his teeth. His face was so pale and blurred, fair the way it was when he was still a baby and hadn't been taken into the sunshine yet. A dog romped by and stopped to sniff at the base of the slide. An older boy on a bicycle whirred past, and the children in the sand both looked up to watch him go.

Rob Murdock came creeping around the corner of the street in his squad car. Two teenagers, a boy and a girl in torn blue jeans and white T-shirts, held hands as they walked off into the trees.

Bo had turned toward me. I could hear the rustle and crunch of his boots in the grass. I slipped behind a broad, blighted elm and pressed my hands hard against the bark so that it pinched and dug in at my palms. I took a cautious peek around the tree, and the bark snagged at my hair.

Bo had stopped to clean his pick. He was hunkered down, pulling the bits of paper off its long, sharp point and cramming them into his already half-full bag. It didn't look like he had seen me yet.

When I turned to sneak off farther into the cover of the trees, a child watched me curiously—I couldn't quite tell whether it was a boy or a girl; its hair was short and it's overalls were smudged. I must have looked odd. I wondered if maybe the child knew who I was. I smiled to show that I was harmless, anyway, and brushed away the bits of bark that had come off and clung to my hands when I had pressed them up against that old elm like that, and then I walked purposefully on out of the park. One time I turned around and took a quick look back over my shoulder, and Bo was standing there in the sand with his legs astride and his hands on his hips, watching me go. The children had all fled.

He looked just like a scarecrow.

When I got home, I went out back into the garden and I brought in some vegetables—tomatoes, a cucumber, lettuce. I cleaned them there at the kitchen sink. I telephoned Lacey, and she told me that Bo hadn't been up there yet; it was too early. She promised me that when he did arrive, she'd be sure and have him call.

I went upstairs. I made my bed and tidied the bathroom. I brushed my teeth and combed the bark out of my hair. There were dark splinters of beard in the sink from when Bo had shaved that morning.

The fan was on, rustling things up in his room. I flipped the switch, and the house was still.

I made up Bo's bed and stashed his dirty clothes in the hamper by the closet door. There was a photo of Lacey Tooker in a flowered cloth frame on the dresser. It was just like the one that Gunar had given to Ted Neeley and called Neva Jolene, shot before Lacey went away, when she was still only a high school girl, probably not even pregnant yet. She hadn't looked much different then, I thought. The same long, dark hair. Maybe she had lost some weight and hardened up. She had always been beautiful enough to take your breath away.

I set the picture back down on Bo's dresser and went down into the kitchen and phoned the Tooker Place again. Yes, Lacey told me, Bo was up there now. No, he was just fine. She had told him to call, and he had said that he would, but it must have slipped his mind. He was in the garage working on the storm window frames, painting them bright white.

I sliced up the tomatoes and the cucumber, and my hands were shaking so I cut my thumb on the knife. Blood welled and dripped, a meandering red river against the clean white porcelain of the kitchen sink. I wrapped a paper towel around my thumb and piled the vegetables into a sandwich for my lunch. They were still warm from the sun. I went up front into the sunroom—the room where the Doctor had examined and consoled his patients, until he died and I brought in my plants—and I sat there on the chaise lounge to eat. The heat closed in on me, the blood from my cut seeped, and I fell asleep.

I dreamed of elephants, and wild animals, and salamanders, and dogs.

When I woke, all I could do at first was just lie there, looking at my plants. They were so green. The violets were dusty; nectar beaded and glistened on the waxy white flowers of the hoya; the gardenia was in full bloom, and its fragrance was heavy on the air. A fly buzzed greedily around the crumbs on my plate on the floor.

I went into the kitchen and splashed water on my face again. I could feel the fabric grid that had been pressed into my cheek as I slept. I looked out the window above the sink at my steaming garden. Then over my shoulder, down the hall, toward the stairs that led upstairs, past the bedrooms to the door that opened up to the attic where . . .

That door had been shut tight.

I never meant to fall asleep.

I dialed Lacey's number again then, but the telephone just rang and rang and rang and no one answered and no one picked it up.

The dread that had been building in me, so slow and so sure and so steady, flipped up into soaring, sudden panic. I shivered; I was as cold as if I had been standing barefoot in the deep white snow, up to my ankles in the icy, midwinter water of the Wizen River.

My hands were shaking, and I squeezed them into fists, hard, "Oh," I was moaning, "No . . ."

I was slamming out through the back door, tumbling down the steps, bruising my bare feet on the gravel of the drive, to my car. I drove up the hill, recklessly rounding the curve past Phoebe's ruined tree, to the Tooker Place.

The storm windows were on the grass in the yard; their fresh white paint glistened in the sun.

The swing on the porch stirred in the breeze. I could see that Bo had painted over that ragged bare patch that Phoebe had picked clean the day she came back home from California without Lacey. When I pushed the front door open, white paint left a print on my palm.

Inside it was quiet, like no one was at home. So still. So cool. Phoebe's rooms folded out into each other, doors open, windows gaping, yawning, empty, abandoned, forsaken, lost.

Mrs. Boots would be asleep, drugged and snoring, upstairs at the back of the house.

Lacey might have taken John out for a walk in the woods.

Bo would be in the garage, whistling through his teeth, cleaning his brushes or mixing up more paint.

There would be wild raspberries for the ice cream after supper.

Or—and this is what I was thinking, this is what I was afraid of, this is what I imagined I would see—they were all of them at home. Lacey and Bo, caught up, entwined in the embrace that he had dreamed of . . .

She on her back, naked, long-limbed, her skin like china, smooth and white, lovely. Her eyes wide open, and blue, rolled back like Phoebe's at her most exasperated. A pretty silk scarf—one I might recognize, because maybe it would be mine—wrapped around her neck, tangled in the gold chain that she always wore—Jack had given it to her on her sixteenth birthday—and that scarf wrapped around so mean and tight, digging into her flesh, cutting bruises in her skin.

Blood blooming like wild redflowers on the walls and on the rug.

Bo lying sprawled on top of her, his face nestled sweetly in against her breasts. The grass-green baseball cap perched on the table nearby. A pair of surgical scissors on the floor, a glint of metal, just beyond Bo's grasp. Clutched in his right hand, a long lock of Lacey's dark hair. Blood seeping and spreading from the wounds on his back.

I might scream for John, calling "John! John! John!" over and over, a litany, a rhythm, a song.

And then the stillness would settle in again, like a blanket, muffling, suffocating, and soft.

Later I would find John, there in the kitchen, huddled in the corner, hunched down upon himself, his head pressed against his bony knees, his thin arms wrapped tightly around his legs. And rocking, rocking, and moaning there all alone in the sunny room, holding the pick that he might have used to try to save his mother's life by taking my boy Bo.

That wasn't how it happened. There wasn't anybody there. Lacey and John had gone out. Casey was still downtown. Bo, overcome by the heat, crippled by a headache, had put down his brushes and quit for the day. He had given up and gone home.

I did find Mrs. Boots, in her bed, sound asleep, drugged, carried away from her pain on the wings of her medication. The bottle of pills was there on the bedside table. Brown plastic, with a tight-fitting, childproof white cap.

Next to the lamp, an opened magazine. An ashtray overflowing. A glass of water. The pills. Easily within reach.

Where Bo could have found them if he had been looking.

195

If he thought he needed them. If he had known that they were there. Where Bo could have taken them, without anyone noticing right away. Where Bo could have sneaked up, after everyone else left, watched Mrs. Boots sleep, her bony face nestled in the pillow, lips fluttering as she breathed, spittle gathering in the corners of her mouth, drugged, painless, her gnarled fingers clasped against her breast. He could have reached out and taken the pills. He could have poured them out into his pocket, held them there in his hand, run them through his fingers like a rosary—release, relief, salvation—and gone home.

He had tried to kill himself once already. Everybody knew. No one would be surprised to hear that he had tried again. And this time . . .

I shook out a handful of the capsules into a tissue and folded it up, gently, softly, like a flower, cradled in my palm.

Bo was in the kitchen, his head buried in his hands, rocking, swaying with the pain. He didn't hear me come in. He didn't look up, until I touched him, and then he smiled, his hands clenched into fists against his cheeks. His eyes were watery and red. His face was wrenched up into a grimace of what must have been excruciating pain.

"My head," he said, through his teeth. When Bo was little, he would moan, rocking on his heels, complaining.

He cried too much, the Doctor said. "Alvays to have his vay dis boy, he cries."

I poured a glass of milk for him and turned away to the sink. My back to him. He wasn't watching. He didn't care. He had his elbows on the table, his hands against his face. I opened Mrs. Boots's capsules and emptied them—three, five, ten—watching, entranced, as the powdered crystals of the drug piled up, spread, thickening, and then sank, heavy, like sand, into the swirling milk.

Outside the window my garden was wild with color. Vines burdened with fruit—melons and squash. The air thick with the fragrance of the flowers.

196

Like Blue, I was thinking. This is how they did it. Just like Lacey's Blue.

When I gave him the glass, Bo held it in his palms. He put it up to his forehead and rolled it back and forth across his skin, soothed by the coolness, eased by the chill. And then he drank it down. He tilted his head back. The brim of his green cap pointed straight up, his Adam's apple bobbed in his throat as he swallowed. The scars under his chin were tangled and tortured and wild.

I helped him, stumbling, upstairs. He smelled of sweat and fear, pain. His hands were cold. I took off his shoes and tucked him down into his bed. Fluffed his pillow, kissed his cheek. I stood by the window, watching him as his eyelids drooped and his breathing slowed. I turned on the fan, and as I left I closed the door.

Later Lacey and John would come in together and see that Bo had left, gone for the day. Later they would discover that some of Mrs. Boots's painkillers and sleeping pills were missing, stolen, gone. At first they would think that she . . .

Later Casey would call and ask about Bo.

"We heard he wasn't feeling well," Casey would say. "Lacey said that he went home."

Later I would go in, quietly, as if to check on him. I would reach out and tangle my fingers in and through Bo's soft hair. The scars on his throat would glimmer, thin and tangled, worming through the surface of his skin. Bo would be sleeping.

Later, Bo would not be mine.

I always believed that to lose a child would be the one thing in this world I could never bear. I couldn't see how it was that people went through the death of a child and still continued to live themselves. To get up in the morning, eat breakfast, go to work, take showers and drive cars, read papers and watch television and sleep. I thought that it would be a loss too heavy and insufferable, too hard. I believed that sadness and sorrow could kill you. I knew that it could rob your sleep. Keep you up at night, in a chair by the window, smoking cigarettes and staring out at the night. I thought that pain could make you die.

But now I understand that as our children get older, as they grow up, they also grow away from us. They drop like ripe fruit. They become something else, unto themselves, other. Every day that goes by drives on the distancing, pushing out, further, until, finally, even our children, our own flesh and blood, babies that grew within and kicked and squirmed and fought for a first breath, become like anything else. Anyone else.

Other. Elsewhere.

It's been ten years now since that summer when Phoebe died and Lacey Tooker came home. One hundred years since Weary Shires married Lucy. Forty since my mother left me. Thirty-two since my father died. Oh, I know what people are saying to each other, out of the way, where I won't be able to hear. They shake their heads, frowning, clucking.

"Poor thing. Poor Annie D.," they whisper.

They feel sorry for me. They sympathize. They pity my situation. They think they understand what they believe to be my pain.

What was it? Why?

If I could, I would . . .

What if I hadn't done enough? There wasn't time. There was too little. It was too late. Too far away. Too long ago.

I did what I could. What else is there?

Daniel and Lucy and Weary Shires have all been dead. Harley Plant, with them, is buried beneath the fields of corn. Mona is either dead or she's not, but anyway she is gone. Dr. Diettermann has found some peace, somewhere. Phoebe and Jack. Neva Jolene and Gunar. And Bo.

I did the only thing that I could think to do. They would have understood. All of them. Even Bo. They would have had to agree. It was for the best. It was the only way.

Maybe the winters seem that much colder and darker to me now. The snow piles up, deeper and more difficult. The

198

summer heat is more deadening. The autumn wane is a greater sorrow every year.

The people in and around Wizen River don't need to lock up their houses at night anymore. They're safe. There are no murderers here. Years ago, I saw to that.

Their daughters and their wives feel free to stroll the streets of town unafraid. Everywhere else in the world violence thumps and pounds its way into the lives of people who don't expect it and are never prepared. I see it every day, on the news.

Not in Wizen River. Not here.

The kids still find their own kind of comfort and closeness under the trees in Center Park, but they seem so much more serious about it all now. As if their lives depended on their love.

John Tooker Boots is among them—nineteen years old, as handsome as his father ever was, and as skittish now, too—with a pretty little girl who clings to him with a desperation that he does not recognize or see.

Casey and Lacey and John live up at the Tooker Place with Mrs. Boots, who is truly helpless now and has a housekeeper of her own, a nurse, to care for her. They had the house repainted—a bright robin's egg blue.

Lacey brings me things—presents, offerings, gifts. Jars of honey, jelly, perfume, books and magazines and soap.

"I saved your life," I want to tell her. "I protected you," I'd like to say. "You owe that you're alive to me."

But I keep quiet. I say nothing. She has no need to know.

I've kept the picture that John drew that night of Neva Jolene. I've had it framed, and it hangs in the kitchen on the wall. Her face in it is beautiful—a kaleidoscope of color, the swirling bright vision of a boy.

Me, I'm all alone. The new doctor tells me that I have a bad heart. I'm not surprised to hear it. My heart is old, broken and worn down.

I take yellow and green pills all day long, and that does something for it, but I don't know what.

I sit by the window, in the Doctor's chair, dressed in my

old overalls that flop and drape around my body, making it look even smaller and more frail than it really is.

I finger the burn-holes in the fabric, picking at the fluff, tearing it away.

Outside the air is nippy with an early frost, and the breezes that brush the trees carry with them the smell of burning leaves.

There is black dirt squeezed in under my nails from the garden that I've just dug up and turned back for the winter freeze.

It's only that I'm old. Sometimes the children will come by to taunt me, just the way they used to do to Nellie Grace Simpson. I remember that at one time all I wanted in the world was to end up just like her. I've heard the children call me crazy, but I'm not. It's only that I'm old.

I loved them all too much, is what. I did what I thought would work to make them happy; I tried to keep them safe.

If you touch the petals of a gardenia to your lips, it will brown and wither and die in your hands. Just to touch it—the softest, most loving caress, a kiss—just to come too close, is to kill its beauty and destroy forever its fragrance and its grace. To love it more than it can bear.

"Don't look at me," Gunar said. "Don't touch me. Don't you stare."

Satis.